T0077813

The Unsung
Heroine

The Unsung Heroine

Anshu Chhetri

PARTRIDGE
A Penguin Random House Company

To order additional copies of this book, contact
Partridge India
000 800 10062 62
orders.india@partridgepublishing.com

www.partridgepublishing.com/india

Contents

Clouds come floating into my life, no longer to carry rain or usher storm, but to add colour to my sunset sky.

Rabindranath Tagore

For my Baba, who inspired me to write and believed in my ability and also motivated me to never give up.

For my late Bara (Uncle), I hope I made you feel proud.

Acknowledgements

My deepest thanks to:
God, my sole strength.
Sano Phupu and Phupaju
(Younger Aunt and Uncle) for guidance.
My Aama for her blessings.
Karen Jimenez, my publishing consultant.
My friends, the active listeners.

One

From the days of my early childhood I was always in search of the better pursuits of my life. In one such stories of my Grandma, she had described about the boy who had the magic lamp, for him life would be so easy I would think and It would be indeed, when he would rub the lamp Genie would appear in a jiffy and then his famous lines would echo before the poor lad "your wish is my command "and perhaps the boy would effulge in joy and without any hard labour he would be rich. I wished to live such grand life too but unfortunately such lamp was never in my fortune; all those were tales from the ages. Was there anything like Genie? I certainly did not know and yet I never asked my Grandma too who would always snort a chuckle at any questions like such at the end of her magical stories. Back then I lived a happy life in one of the cosy huts of Nepal until I became the eldest of my other three sisters.

A time came when my grandma stopped to share the ancient tales, one night she woke me up, I would sleep beside her, I felt her head she was perspiring, she was cold, and I lighted a lamp in hurry. In the faint light she kissed my hand and whispered my name softly, I tried listening even in the pin- drop silence but her voice was so weak that even my ears could not reach her, she died in my lap, and my tears touched her cheeks it looked like she cried with me.

My two sisters Renu and Parvati were still a kid when my mother conceived again. Baba always required a helping hand, to help him carry the shovel and dig with him the land that would dry and crack in the unsuitable season. I was born a daughter, the family comprised of five which would soon become six. His hard labour bore no fruits and after my youngest sister was born we left the village, I was six years old then and my two other siblings were four, my little sister Neelu still cradled in the hands of my Aama. At first a refugee but we soon accustomed ourselves in the tea estate where my Baba started to work as a gardener in the 'Kothi' of Bara sahib, the local name given to his huge bungalow who was also the owner of the tea gardens. The garden had the most exotic flowers; the entire area was therefore filled with sublime colours which looked like a heaven on earth, the red and yellow bougainvilleas would entice the passerby. It hung humbly, swept the streets with its long gracious thin branches that would make me remember one of the stories of grandma which was about the beautiful palace garden, but my imagination failed before the beauty that sahib's garden carried, pristine and pure. I would boast every time I walked by that way sometimes alone and many a times with Arpana. We were of the same age, the many similarities that we had actually strengthened our friendship to such an extent that we became the cordial friends after our first meeting in weekly bazaar. While bargaining with one of the sellers she stood by me in amazement and also supported in voicing together. With polite 'thank you' we became friends and in the free time from our daily chores we started to spent time together. We had the dreams of luxuriating in the 'kothi' like that of Bara sahib which was so magnificent and painted in white. As it was built amidst the green tea gardens the white building glistened like pearl inside a mossy ocean. Tall green hedges were the boundary around along with the big Iron Gate. There was no gate keeper as such yet no body dared to enter because of the two German shepherds with large bodies and black eyes, their barks where enough to shoo any trespasser out but the other reason was everybody respected Sahib, he was a generous being who loved his labours with a true heart and helped everybody in difficult period of time.

One day Baba took all four of us to visit sahib's garden, I was mesmerised by its beauty that was so divine and secretly I praised my Baba's hands too. Flowers of various colours bloomed everywhere, stones painted in fine colours were arranged perfectly in a row in the places where required. I did not join in the Ring a Ring a Rose's play of my sisters rather just sat in one corner and enjoyed every single thing that belonged to sahib. Baba seemed to be nowhere and I did not bother to look for him either. One big swing was kept somewhere in the middle and I wondered do sahib have children? If so then where are they? I did not ponder over such thoughts for long but sat on the swing and hummed a soft tune that I had learnt from Arpana. She would be equally happy like me if she was here but never mind I was in all happy minds to share with her my wonderful experience in sahib's garden. After so long all four of us were out together with Baba, I can't even recall about my last outing. Being the eldest sister I had to sacrifice more, this would always pinch my heart when my desires were given no worth, I had to remain satisfied on everything that was left over by my sisters, and they went to school while I did not. Sometimes I would just scribble my name on a sheet of paper

'Meera', the only word I knew, my sister Parvati had taught me to write and all day long I would just write the same word and when nothing more would come in my empty brain I would crumple the page and throw in the bin in disgust. Life was so monotonous, I no more wanted to carry water from the nearby tank, give bath to my sisters and help them to comb their hair and carry Neelu and wipe her snotty nose when Mother would escape from her daily chores and engage in bitching about the entire village leaving me behind with everything. Thankfully Neelu had grown up by now and she too went to the same school where everyone went. Yet I never complained Baba about my illiteracy, he was already laden with enough burdens and I never wanted to make his life more miserable, I remained silent wishing that the tide will slowdown and once again happy days will return back.

One day in the late afternoon I met with Arpana. She looked overwhelmed, she came towards me and pulled my ear near her mouth and started to whisper. We were in the local shop and the people's gaze fell into us but nobody could hear her plan. I gave her a confusing look, her face dropped and suddenly the radiant smile faded. With much anticipation she said

"Please say yes".

How could I deny to her innocence and without thinking much I just nodded my head.

"Will Ramu kaka agree?" She questioned.

"I don't know" I replied.

"He will surely Meera, he will not deny you."

"I hope so".

And we both left with hopes and expectations. She lived in another lane, away from mine.

Two

The first thing that I noticed when I went back home was the cycle that Baba had parked safely in the small veranda of our home. I ran in joy and embraced it. It shone in the beams of the sun. My sisters were back, they went to the school run by the government where everything was free from books to uniforms and even mid day meals were provided. I was never sent to school, Baba took my side when I broke down to tears but before my mother's angry agitation nothing could work and hence I was made my sister's keeper. Renu said something to her twin Parvati in the faintest voice as possible and they began to laugh in chorus. I did not pay any heed for what their talks were about rather remembered about Arpana's plan that suddenly made my heart beat faster. I went towards the kitchen and took out the things that I had brought from the shop. Baba was eating food in a hurry. I tried to frame a correct sentence as often I faltered while speaking to him. We all sat together, I placed the plates gently and served food with one eye fixed on Baba as I had to seek his permission. Small beads of sweat appeared on my forehead, I wiped them with my hand.

Mustering my courage I spoke about the plans refusing the eye contact. He did not speak a word and everybody remained silent too. I felt so awkward; it was for the first time that I was placing any request in front of him. I could only hear him snort; he finished the food, washed his hands and noiselessly left the room. I waited much longer for his answer, for him to call me and respond to what I had asked him but he continued to remain quiet. We were done eating, I concluded by assuming that I doomed Arpana's plan and obviously I did. Tiny tears trickled down from my eyes as I scrubbed the utensils out in an open area, at that moment I felt dejected, I could never live life on my own terms, my anger rose to a fit towards Baba. All I could do was be sorry for myself and make a 'tch-tch' sound; there was only the room for self pity for myself.

"Meera Didi, Baba is calling you." Neelu called me later. She was panting and her tiny anklets jingled as she ran away in haste. She brought me back from my trance; I was already shaken with wrath and hatred. Unwillingly I went with little curiosity.

"Calm down" I told to myself.

I saw Baba before the small wooden gate where he was smoking 'Biri', a cigarette like substance. However it looked different in colour and the size was small too. He puffed it one more time and threw away the butt once he saw me approaching.

"Here", he said and gave away the keys of his new cycle which Sahib had gifted him the very morning. I was surprised and speechless too, he took me in cloud nine. I looked at him with teary eyes but this time I had the tears of extreme happiness.

"Be on time and take care of the cycle. I don't want to see any scratches".

"But Baba, I am going tomorrow in the afternoon".

"You can keep it from now. But mark my words be on time".

He completed the sentence and left for work. I was overjoyed. I showered many kisses on the keys. I was going with Arpana in a day out. I visualised us riding between the lush tea gardens, we would bump, would fall even but never mind we would cherish every moment of our everlasting friendship.

Three

I woke up in the peak of dawn for at least five minutes I had lied on the bed weaving the thread of my own fantasies, sometimes twisting and turning in excitement. From the deep sleep Parvati had showed her disgust as she said

"Hush didi, don't disturb"

My mind was unstable, I had grown impatient. Never mind I got down from the bed and left my two sisters sleeping I went out and sat beneath the old jackfruit tree. The gentle breeze passed by my ears, flocks of white birds flew above me, the shrill chirpings of the birds sound pleasant to my ears, and I closed my eyes and lived in the moment. I could never really coin out the meaning of 'Rangamati', the name of the tea estate where we lived but whatever it was, it definitely was one of the best handiworks of the almighty, everything around was merged in green from fruit trees to tea gardens and from shrubs to bushes. The seasonal river flowed from both the sides and in monsoon the level rose and if not careful while crossing, the river showed no mercy and carried any mortal and devoured on it whose only swollen body would remain in the end with no life which sometimes was even difficult to find. In one such tempestuous storm of the previous year accompanied by rain and hailstorms the entire village trembled with fear, we huddled together in our houses. Later when the situation was calm and everybody were back to normal Baba returned back in the evening with the news of the sad demise of Milan Phupa. He drowned in the river while returning back from the fishing spot, he was alone, and nobody could save him. Sadly Arpana lost her beloved father whom she adored immensely and being a single child she was the beloved daughter of her Baba.

The two magpies stood on the branches of the tree, they had remain unnoticed until one of them proudly pooped on my shirt, the smell was terrible but it was a sign of good luck too, the hoary tale passed on from the ages, before I could chase them off they by themselves flew away to some faraway land. After spending half an hour I cleaned my shirt and hurried towards the village spring, I carried two 'ghailas' a kind of earthern pot but generally made out of silver or brass and one small tumbler. The village women and few dainty girls had already occupied much space; some were busy scrubbing their bodies while some where waiting for their turns to fill their empty belongings. I washed my face and splashed some cool water on my half drowsy eyes. I always hated to stand on a long queue, yet I stood for some time chewing the Tulsi leaves. My time finally arrived and I did everything in a hurry because I knew that I was late.

The white trails of smoke had fogged the air; it gave me a clear indication that she had risen up from her bed and was perhaps waiting for me to follow her commands obediently, place a saucer on the stove, and blow my lungs out to ignite the fire and serve tea to Baba which cleverly she would carry to him to prove once again that she is the ideal wife in front of his eyes. I had spent my entire childhood days in the absence of my mother who had given me birth but she never could replace her, when one day I noticed her saving the big chicken flesh for my sisters, before me in my plate was thick broth and the skin and later when I asked for a flesh she whacked me at the side of my ear and took advantage of my Baba's absence. I never argued out of fear of being rejected. My biological mother had died out of childbirth and somewhere I carried the guilt of her death. I felt that my birth was a curse on her; unknowingly I was responsible for her death. I know no history about how my Baba had found my stepmother who day by day began unveiling her true colours but only before me. Either by punishing me for no reason and making me work like a slave.

Just like I had assumed, I prepared the tea, she took it to my father, and I engaged myself in the other chores. Soon the house was empty with only her and me, my sisters were off too school, and Baba too had left for work.

"Meera" she called me from inside.

I hurried my pace to respond but I cried out loudly at her in utter disgust.

"How dare you?" She had held my slate which Parvati had secretly brought for me to teach me the alphabets. I wished I had not written my name above.

"So you have become a thief now? Shameless creature." she spat the words out from her filthy mouth just like a poisonous snake that spits the venom and hurts without care, sometimes even kills. She blamed me for stealing her daughter's slate which I had not. It was useless to justify the truth before her, she was one such stubborn lady who always denied the truth and every time wanted to prove that she is only right.

I gave her a cold look and said "I did not steal". I felt like crying but I controlled my emotions. Tears show weakness and I knew that I was not weak. She began muttering in rage, I left silently and took out the keys and cycled down the slopes to meet Arpana.

Four

All through my way I wondered how she knew about the slate. Last night Renu had asked me for it, her complaints were against the teacher whom she called 'Gabudaley' which means a man who is dull and dumb, she could never understand what he taught, most of the times she found him gibberish. In one such class when she felt the new chapter was difficult to learn and even the teacher was a complete disappointment she hurled her slate down in the plastered floor in anger, it cracked and she had borrowed from me. Perhaps she forgot to take it with her today to school. Nobody cared much and it was on my so called mother's hand today before which the slate had remained hidden for so long beneath my pillow.

I tried to find peace of mind so I pedalled fast, though at first my feet struggled to acquire an exact position but later I could, In the faint light of the sun I could see my shadow ahead of me. The sky was clear and it looked like a canopy but extraordinarily beautiful and high so high that even the birds could not reach. A stray dog was all in fears when I followed it, it began to run here and there and my way formed a zigzag pattern. No sooner it dissolved in one of the lanes so swiftly that I could just catch its glimpse. Arpana stood in a distance, I recognised her yellow skirt that had ruffles in the edges, and I was an ardent admirer of them. Her Baba had gifted her and she always felt special whenever she wore it. She had round black eyes, long tresses that rested perfectly on her shoulder, she was lean unlike me. She could sing and it was indeed her prized possession. She longed to be a mother sometimes and have her own children because she wanted to sing them melodious lullabies; 'her babies would surely be lucky' I would think silently.

On reaching her I observed a small bag that she had carried. I had no clue what was in store inside, I preferred to stay ignorant and wait for her to reveal the mystery.

"So ready?" she asked me excitedly.

"Yes. I am." I answered.

She climbed on her cycle and soon she was on the lead. I pedalled this time with more energy. We crossed the narrow lanes where kids with grimy face frolicked and ran with dogs by pulling their tails; we pressed the 'tring tring' bell when required. It was enjoyable to bump in the potholed areas as well. By mistake the puddle water splashed a little on my face when Arpana tried to overtake me. She did not notice, she was in fun mood and I chose to remain quiet. I did not want to complain and spoil the moment. The hustle bustle was over and we reached the outskirts now that had its own aura. Green mountains were clearly visible and even the roads that crawled through the valleys. No more tea gardens but just an empty vast land filled with sand, mud and boulders and in them danced the river which had decreased in volume now because of the scanty rain that poured down only when the clouds darkened after the extreme heat of the day. There were neither vegetation nor rice fields but just green meadows where wild flowers and weed had appeared. Overall the sight was picturesque and in no time we both parked our cycles and wandered around like the tourists.

I remembered those bygone days in Nepal when along with my clan of friends we tried to explore the thick woods, though small in age but we would carry lion's courage and set our foot forward hooting and howling and then our voices would echo and the birds would fly over our heads their wings would flap and flutter. Till dusk we would collect the wild mushrooms and berries to take back home, thorns surely pricked, there would be scratches too but when my family would eat in delight and my Baba would pronounce 'shyaabaash', it would make me forget everything.

"Look Mira"

I looked at the direction where Arpana showed with her long fingers. A peacock had spread its colourful feathers that dazzled as it began dancing. It stood much distance away from us; but we could see it clear as there were no trees to hide it but it stood on the soft meadow. We were amazed seeing the creation of the supreme power. The river gave us a call by its enigmatic sound that was so distinct in the noiseless nature. The stones of irregular shapes could be seen in the crystal clear visage of the water. I scooped my hand inside by joining the two palms together and took out some water that looked so pure. It was virgin with no impurities.

"Can we drink?" Arpana asked.

"Yes, we can" I answered gaily.

We finished drinking and I quenched my thirsty mind. I dipped my feet inside and even Arpana did taking a cue from me.

"Do you want to hear a story?" I said.

"What story?" She questioned.

"Would you like to listen?"

"Surely" she replied curiously.

I told her one of the favourite stories from Grandma about 'Soonkesari Rani', the queen with Golden hair who would take bath in the early dawn at the river, her long locks would flow down, somewhere from a small hole sun peeked and in its reflection her golden long hair would shine. She was the epitome of beauty and many kings from various regions were her suitors but she chose the one who was lame. The lame king was brave at heart and was a courageous warrior too; he was a great handler of sword. Queen loved him and they lived a blissful life. One day the tragedy took place, the queen was exploited by a hunter who watched her bathe, her throat was slit by his scythe and the queen died in the pool of blood. When the King heard the news he was devastated, he could not bear the loss of his beloved

Queen. He sent his men to find the hunter who belonged to the nearby village. The hunter was caught and he was brought before the King who remained calm and asked for the reason why he killed her.

"Meera, Please continue"

I grinned at her, she was so much interested in my story that she even did not let me to strike a worm out from my shirt that crawled and nearly reached my bare neck.

I continued my story further and I described about the hunter who was in his youth and was very charming. He accepted the allegation that was onto him but he also confessed that the Queen lured him though indirectly, he grew lustful with the physical appearance which was so alluring. The Queen had sculpted body, her curves were marvellous. His head was parted from his body later. The king was never relieved and always mourned her death.

"What happened next?" Arpana asked.

"My Grandma concluded the story here. I don't know what the ending was". I replied.

"Is it a true story?"

"Perhaps" I said.

The small pebble formed the transparent rings when Arpana threw it inside the shallow water. In return of my story she sang a song that soothed my ears and I even remembered the few lines

"Chiso batash le malai sandesh ke lyaayo

Aaja pheri malai yaha jiuna mann lagyo"

"The cool breeze has arrived again with a message and I get inspired to relive my life again".

Her mellifluous voice was truly gifted. And the sun faded, sky changed its colour, birds flew back to their nests, we finished munching the freshly plucked Guavas which was inside her bag. Lastly, the day came to an end.

Five

The lightning flashed through the thin curtains of the window, I was not asleep, my sisters were but when the clouds collided with each other and the sound frightened those who were awake, Renu in fear said

"Didi, I am scared"

I held her tightly, I always slept in the middle they felt safe in my warmth, I pulled the blanket unto our chins, there was heavy downpour outside. The frogs croaked in unison, we all cuddled together. Caressing Renu's hair I murmured

"Sleep in peace. Don't worry".

She did not speak. The room illuminated in the bolts of swift currents from sky, the lamp was flickering, it was not being able to survive in the wind yet it died because of the wind gushing inside from the small cracks and holes of our house which my Baba could not repair in all these years, feeding such a large number was no easy and sometimes he too indulged in gambling, one or two times he earned twice he offered, he lost at one time an inconsiderable amount also. I was always a silent observer. When the rain had stopped I assumed that it was midnight, I lighted the lamp once again and it glowed, I half covered it with my hand and began searching for a small wooden box which was the only treasure I inherited from my Aama. My Grandma had handed over to me. I found it in my trunk where I had kept safely under the clothes and a wide smile ran on my lips. Before opening I wished to myself

"A very Happy Birthday Meera"

Yes it was my birthday; I had become eighteen years old an adult as most of the village women say. The box contained a doll made out of husk, it fitted perfectly inside, Aama had made it long before my birth when she was a teen like me and she always treasured it. She had actually saved it for her offspring. On my each birthday I did the same. The doll had a name even; it was 'Devi', the name of my Aama. I kept the doll back to its place after straightening the pleated frock that it wore. I kissed her goodnight, blew out the lamp and slept between my sisters cosily.

Raajan knocked the door next day; Baba was not at home though he was on a day off still he had gone to sahib's kothi for a reason which he only knew. Only Parvati was with me, my sisters and mother had gone to watch the puppet show which was being shown in the village across the river. Every year a group came from the plains with special arrangements and narrated the story about Raja and

Rani. I had also been there at once with Arpana, the heat was melting and in the open field the show was hosted, half the village had come, a child died due to suffocation in the massive crowd that fought for seats, the mother's frantic search for her kid was heart rending, we couldn't witness the pathetic scene further. Later we resolved that we will never go again. I chose to stay behind because Parvati was not keeping well; she had mild fever.

"Nobody is at home. Come later". I told the man who was in his fifties and I disliked him from the core of my heart.

"When will your Baba come?" he asked with a wicked smile.

He stood in the doorstep and gave me an intent look. He twisted the thick moustache, a crude Ruffian was he.

"I have no idea" I replied.

"Ok child, I will come at night." He said and bid me goodbye.

Raajan was my far relative, he was my Kaka but one day when he fondled my cheeks and tried to come near me I had spat on him in anger. I had left the room in tears and had locked myself for long in the bathroom. Baba thought that I had become notorious; he always respected Kaka for his individuality as he was the so called 'Samaj Sevak' the social worker. Never could Baba find out that Kaka was a man with evil intentions. He was not married but had licentious desires that were easy to notice by the way he always scanned me from top to bottom every time I appeared before them to offer tea. Was it that Baba was acting ignorant about the whole truth? It was a mystery indeed.

I felt Parvati's forehead, temperature had decreased, she looked just like a baby in her sleep, her fair skin and rosy cheeks were flawless, and she was the prettiest among all of us. I sat on the edge of the veranda. Nobody knew I had my birthday, Baba knew it but he never wished me, with sunken face I looked towards the sky, I remembered my Grandma. She always said

"You will see the rainbow. Let the storm pass."

I was deprived of love for which I always yearned. And even God seemed so distant. I felt lost somewhere in the crowd, feigning smile was so easy but I was looking for a genuine smile in my face that could only appear when I was with Arpana or when I could feel a tinge of Baba's love. If Aama was alive in every weary time I could run to her and cry and wipe my tears with the edge of her saree, she would take me to the market and would ask me to have 'piro chana matar' or 'spicy fried lentils' wrapped in the newspaper by the shabby vendor, I could see her laugh and she would keep each details of me and help me to stay strong by teaching various ideals of life. In her absence, I was growing, I wanted to be judged by her and hear her voice say

"Meera, you are not on the right track or I am proud of you"

But she was not here but somewhere far in the sky, that star which I looked at night before closing my eyes. She always watched me sleep.

Baba returned back home late at night, tensed and frustrated, his eyes bulging out, and his face mixed with dirt and oil, it seemed as if he had worked for long hours. He was silent as if in a deep meditation. I had watched the oil lamp burning bright while my sisters were already asleep when I heard the lattice of our wooden gate rattle, It was Baba when I saw his lanky frame drooping low as he entered.

Next morning, I heard voices from the backyard, on peeking I found Baba and Raajan having a heated conversation. He had not come the previous night so he came early morning to poke the already broken heart of Baba by his curt sntences that could give a hard smash on a person's face without raising hand.

"You have two choices Ramu" he exclaimed.

Baba's face was low, he looked around and I quickly hid behind the wall moped with mud and cow dung. The sky was slowly changing its colour, the environment too was responding to its alarm as the birds started to chirp, sun's rays radiated from the Blue Mountains and slowly it was rising up.

"Please have mercy on me". Baba pleaded before him with a face that could arouse anybody's sympathy.

"We all live in a selfish world. Nobody is anybody's well wisher." He said.

"Will you give me some time?" Baba asked.

"One week and if you don't manage to fulfil you know what you have to pay in place of the debt."

"I will manage; you will never get what you want."

"That we will see in time".

The entire conversation was very confusing. I could not ask Baba, he would never tell me the truth. All I knew was that we were on huge debt.

Six

The days were passing by. Time was running short. Baba was worried; he would look at me with miserable eyes, he was in grief which he was constantly hiding from all of us. I did not know whether mother knew about it or not, Baba always suppressed his emotions that would make him more burdened.

In the middle of the night the large footsteps woke me and Parvati, the sound was so clear and apparent.

"Didi, what is going on?" Parvati asked.

"I don't know"

I was equally inquisitive like her. Both of us saw Baba driving past in Sahib's car with few men. Something was going wrong; difficulties had come in the threshold. Silently I prayed that everything be fine. We couldn't do anything but wait for the morning to arrive. Later in the evening, when Baba returned back he broke the news that Sahib had passed away, he died and his death itself was so uncertain. Sahib was ailing from many days; he had nobody by his side not even his relatives who stayed in some far corner of the country. He had no parents and was not married either, all through his life he lived alone but he enjoyed his loneliness, he would go for hunting, fishing and oftentimes he would read books. His thirst for knowledge was prominent from his collection of books that were fat and some even huge too. In the open area he had a small house built of glasses where in rows books were stacked and it was here, where he would organise tea parties and book reading ceremonies.

Baba said that he had a minor fever the day he was called and last night after the dinner Sahib retired to bed, he woke Ramesh his housekeeper when he howled in pain, and Sahib was on the floor struggling hard to get up. Baba was called and they took him to the hospital but before they could reach Sahib breathed his last breath in the middle of the way. It surely was heart breaking to lose Sahib and more importantly for Baba who shared a bond of brotherhood. He remained silent for rest of the days and one fine morning he called me and said to get dressed. He was taking me to market; a vehicle would come to take us.

"But whose vehicle?" I asked in amazement.

"Get dressed" he said.

Baba was taking me out leaving rest of my sisters behind and this was not going into my system, we had never gone anywhere, only two of us. Back in my mind I was happy, we finally could spend some time alone, I would ask him questions about his past, my Aama, how she looked like, my childhood days and many more. I put on the only good dress that I had in my trunk, combed my long hair and divided it into two braids, applied some talcum powder and sprinkled in my body to smell good and probably to grab attention in the marketplace. My sisters looked at me intently, were they jealous? Well, I did not know. I glanced at the mirror one more time, I carried Devi with me, the doll made out of husk by Aama in a small bag, then the family would be complete, I carried the purse and waited for Baba outside in the veranda, mother stood in the doorstep and my sisters followed me too.

"Didi where are you going"? Neelu asked.

"I have no idea." I answered.

"Can we come with you"?

"Next time". I answered and held her hand tightly.

We walked for a while. Baba was quiet the whole time, his eyes were down. I was tongue-tied too, in a distance a vehicle came in view that would carry us to the market. Jaigaon was not so far away, it was half an hour journey from the tea estate. I had been there once when the local fair had created an entertaining havoc in the village and we too had joined the crowd. The big merry go rounds, cotton candies, chaats and bhelpuris and the lights all around had enticed the people. Arpana bought a big gemmed stud that she gladly wore in the fair and wherever she went be it a local market, she did not mind when the hawkers would stare or the fishmonger delayed in cutting the 'Rohu' in pieces when the man's eye would dim as her stud sparkled so bright in the sunlight.

"Baba, where are we going?" I questioned breaking an awkward silence that had existed with us for more than a while.

"Jaigaon, you are going with Raajan". He replied.

I was taken aback by the news. It was completely unexpected not from Baba whom I always felt that Raajan wanted to win over me, my body. What had compelled him to take such unpredicted decision? I wanted to scream, create a hue all around, hold Baba's leg and plead for mercy. Would he listen to me or walk forward not pitying me for even once even if I dragged on the mud and receive cuts and scratches on my knee and hands and shed tears of disapproval?

I did not speak a word neither he waited for my response because very soon he entered a narrow lane from where Raajan came in view. He was happy and hid his one hand in the pocket of his khaki shirt which was buttoned from up. I could not stand the way he looked at me curling his moustache he greeted us with a smile and joined his two palms together and uttered 'Namastey'.

"Take care of my daughter" Baba said and he looked at me with eyes that were brimming with tears. I stayed strong; I did not want to cry before Raajan, at least not before him. He was the most hated soul of my life. I was filled only with wrath and fury towards Baba and his tears had no worth now even if it were genuine. He proved to be a coward and a selfish being; if I had no value in his life he too had none in my heart too.

"Forgive me Meera" Baba said.

"Why should I forgive you? Who am I? I was never your daughter. You sold me to this man knowingly. Do you know how shameful his thoughts and desires are? I can never forgive you". I spoke within. I just stood dumbstuck. All I could do was to remain quiet because at that moment I was not in a state of mind to speak. I passed by him with my new master.

Baba cried this time and howled like a kid. I too was carried by emotions but I wanted him to suffer now and beg me to love him once again in the same way as I did if we could ever see each other again.

Seven

Rajaan's house was the most beautiful in the entire neighbourhood which stood erect painted in white, the small Iron Gate in black. The rooms were big and spacious, well furnished walls. A big framed picture of a known freedom fighter was kept on the living room not only to enhance the decor but also it would signify his love for the country and people as he was the so-called 'Samaaj Sevak'. However, the truth was something different, he was a corrupt and all his riches and lifestyle clearly was the sheer evidence.

In such an enormous dwelling, only three of us were the existing individuals. Raajan also had a sister who was visually challenged. Her name was Gayatri, a woman in her early thirties. At first I was in a complete bewilderment by looking at her and observing how much she worked from day to night, she was so familiar with everything and she did not need a support to move around, she truly was a gifted person though she was deprive in one that she could not see. This never could let her stoop low and feel inferior rather she was the backbone of Raajan's life without which he would limp in his every walk of life. When I was first brought in the house I did not know that what would be my identity, a sister, maid or spouse. I was none. I was Meera in front of Gayatri who treated me as her sister and no sooner we became best of friends. The age difference was never a hindrance to our bond. We would remain at house only two of us and we both would put in our effort to set the house in perfect order. She always wanted to see the roses of her own garden which I had planted and every day we sat on the backyard. I watered the plants and the fragrance of the roses would linger in the air and out of excitement, Gayatri would say

"Hey Meera, are the roses alive?"

"Yes, they are red and lively. Do you want to feel them?" I would ask.

"Sure"

And she would feel the tiny petal that I would pluck for her. For a long time she would smell being so delighted and happy enormously.

Raajan often came late at night, sometimes in so much of aggression. His mouth would smell alcohol; in such times it would be very difficult to change the situation into a perfect harmony. In one or two I was beaten when Gayatri would speak on top of her voice to settle the matter and when I interrupted he would push me hard and slang me, my cheeks would turn red after bearing the slaps. Later when he would come back to his senses in the morning he would wake me up in the middle of my deep slumber, his hard unshaved beard touched my cheeks as he would kiss me and cuddle with me. I never could deny when he touched me and fondled with my private parts. After all I was his whore in the house and this I realised when for the first time he asked me to shed my clothes at night after the dinner when I was viewing out of the window. It had rained that night and the heavy downpour had made me homesick. Though I was given a separate room but there was no privacy, I could not even close the door especially during the night-time. A cold hand had touched me from behind; the touch was spine-chilling. When I turned back it was Raajan looking at me with sensual eyes. He acted as if he was comforting me by taking me in his arms and as I was a lonely, desolate and sad soul I embraced him back and began crying with my lungs out. He patted me gently on my back, and then started caressing my hair. I wiped my tears and wanted to loosen myself from his hard grip. My body wanted to stick while my inner core knew that it was wrong. By this time he had already attacked on my virginity. I could not do anything. From then on I became his slave and he my master before whom I could never agitate, If I did he would beat me at first then eye on my sister Renu and he always said that he will bring her here someday. He would conclude himself by saying

"I will wait for the fruit to be ripe for I want to taste it sweet and juicy".

He spoke dirty language, very disgusting to ears, intolerable many a times especially when it would be related to my sister. I was born to be my sister's keeper until Raajan took me away and in those years of togetherness I had never realised how much I loved them as I realised now, I wanted to be their defender, keeping my own life on the tip of sword. Anytime prone to get poked and my life would come to an end. Then I would sleep the most peaceful sleep, free from the shackles of everything, just me and my sweet never ending slumber. I could never imagine my life without Gayatri, I shared my vision with her, and she just listened to the sounds of the birds early morning taking the sips of the steaming hot black tea with extra punch of pepper. I would narrate her names of those birds chirping melodiously. Our conversation would never end, she was a tough lady in Raajan's life but with me she was always so soft. She had to play the character of two in the same house.

Gayatri wanted to fall in love with the person about whom she always fantasized and I wondered shamelessly that her vision would be coloured or dark with lights flickering here and there or would it be black and white? She would always ask me that would she ever find a lover in her life. I was clueless so as her yet I would say

"Of course dear, He will come in a white horse."

And she would smile and say "Now, that is too much".

Eight

The memories haunt now and I wish to see Gayatri again so that we can relive the bygone days of those cherished moments. I am no more with them but have fallen into the darkest pit from where it seems almost impossible to escape. So easily I fell into the trap and now I regret because every second I cry voiceless tears.

Soon after a year Raajan revealed his darker side when one day I tried to pry on his secret conversation and was left awestruck when I heard him say

"Don't worry; she is absolutely fine and healthy. As soon as I hand her to you I want my share, you can even pay me in instalments".

I grew curious to know more about the matter and hurriedly listened to the entire conversation in another phone. I could hear a very gruff male speaking. He inquired about me and said that he wanted me as soon as possible.

Tears started to roll down my cheeks, the world started to revolve around me and covering my mouth with one hand I ran towards Gayatri and narrated the entire story. She held me in her arms and whispered that everything will be fine.

"I don't want to leave you". I protested

"You have to go if you want to be safe". She said.

As according to what we had planned when Raajan was in sleep I decided to climb down from the window because the door was locked and I would escape and go back to my home. Gayatri sat before me and scooped my face in her palm and began sobbing as she bid me goodbye.

I could not suppress my emotions and started to howl loudly. She wiped my tears and warned me about Raajan and to run away as soon as possible. With a small backpack hung on my shoulder I left and gifted her with my most precious companion, the husk doll 'Devi'. But before I could take any step Raajan grabbed my hand and pulled me up again. He was soaked in deep remorse and anger. Without uttering a single word he pulled me by my hair and slapped me. I was thrashed on the ground along with Gayatri who wanted to save me from the brutal abuse. It was for the first time in his life indeed that he raised his hand on Gayatri too.

Next morning I woke up and found myself with wounds and scratches on the floor. I searched for Gayatri but she was not there, not even in the entire house. But I found a man and then I realised that he was the same man whom Raajan wanted his share by offering me to him.

"She looks wonderful even with the cuts and wounds" he commented.

"But she will be more beautiful after the recovery". Raajan answered.

I was in front of the two men whose keen eyes were enough to threaten me. I mustered my courage and asked

"Where is Gayatri?"

"She went away and left you behind". He said.

"No she did not. Where is she?"

"She is gone". He replied.

I held him by the collar and fixed my eyes onto his and screamed so loud because I loved her so much and did not want to hear the news that she is gone somewhere far from me which Raajan only knew.

"Where did you take her?" I asked.

"It is none of your concern." He yelled at me.

I could not witness the sudden disappearance of Gayatri. I just could remember that when Raajan had kicked me hard on my chest I fell into the ground and was totally blacked out. But now it was too late for me to find her because I belonged to the other master now. He took me away with him in a price that he payed to Raajan.

Nine

The city was obviously beautiful unlike the people with whom I was forced to labour. Soon after the sudden disappearance of Gayatri, I was forced to join the troupe that comprised of the people from both the genders who wanted to free themselves from the so called poverty but the truth however was something different. Raajan had hired a pimp that day that appeared so innocent but was a treacherous man. They had signed a covenant. Raajan would help him with the people and he would get a juicy amount in return. And this was the very reason why Raajan was called by him as "Boss".

When we reached the destined place there were two medium sized concrete buildings in front. I tried to look for a company because I felt myself to be lost amidst the crowd and more weird when two bulky men began walking towards us with the expression that was so cruel. We were divided into groups then, each group had five people. I felt as if we were some goods on display for the men to pick and choose anyone depending upon their preferences. The eerie silence was broke by the baby's cry which had been cradling on the arms of its mother. The attention fell on her and the pimp angrily said

"Better get rid of this little pup. You have come here to work not to nurse the infant."

The lady remained quiet but I grew in rage and felt like shooting a stone at his dumb head so that he could realize how precious a baby for a mother is.

"Hey take it away from her". He ordered one of his assistants.

The lady at once kneeled down on her knees and began pleading for sympathy but the baby was snatched from her. Both the mother and the child shed the most painful tears of departure, their cries pierced our hearts too. After that she could never find her baby. She could not overcome her pain and yet ended up in killing herself by consuming poison.

Soon the men began to direct us with the instructions that were obviously not hand written but they knew it by heart and I wondered for how many times they have recited them before us. We had to start our work from the next day with the group which we belonged to and each group had a supervisor too who was given the duty to look after us and provide the pimps with everyday updates of our lives that whether we are doing our tasks properly or not, the date when we would get the wages and if everybody paid their half of the amount to the pimp or not. We were not working for ourselves neither for our families but for them. Our lives were at their hands as we slaves now were relegated to the background.

Next day the work started with full swing. We had a group of two women and three men. To reach Lalitpur from our location would take half an hour and on reaching, we encountered tall buildings that were ready to kiss the blue sky above with their pointed height that looked more like the tentacles of a huge giant. We grouped together in one corner of the wide street and the man who was on the lead began to instruct us. Just then a woman clad in a soiled drape interrupted him by opening the palm and asked for both mercy and penny but received none rather the man pushed her on the ground as he tried to free himself from the grip. She began to cry but it could not disturb the man further and he continued by saying that we were assigned to work together in one of the big mansions of the city of some rich owner.

"Hurry up, now don't waste time". He commanded

All of us like the unarmed soldiers began to follow him and we passed through the wide alleys and narrow lanes and soon witnessed a big house encircled by an area of wide stretch with flowers blooming here and there. It reminded me of Sahib's kothi that had the same aura. I was attracted at once and could not take my eyes off the beauty that the house reflected that had large windows from where the long curtains flowed and when the wind would blow they would look divine as when it would swing in the same rhythm.

We started our work from the early dawn till the dusk. The land and the mansion were owned by a Sardar who had two sons and a bunch of grand children, their mothers and grandmother too. Every day I would notice him, the colour of his turban would change daily. All day he would bask outside tuning to a radio that was as dear to him as most of the time he would spent with it. He never would sip the normal water but lukewarm water that would always contain some amount of ginger and lemon. I had to always place the brass jar before his arrival. I would always be with four kids whose mothers had no time for them but they always made it a point to plant kisses on the cheeks of each individuals. Often I would wonder that were the kisses only the gestures to express love in front of the outsiders or did they actually love them? This way I was aware about the every temperaments of the kids, they would call me "Mia di" as their tiny mouths could not pronounce it well. My favourite among the six was 'Parul', a five years old girl with beautiful curly hairs and round eyes. Her face was as familiar as it would make me remember my little sister 'Parvati'. She would never leave me till I would retire from work and she always had something to give me be it a flower, sweets or a peck on my cheek. When the kids would play she preferred to stay with me, and then her questions would start one after the other.

That day she startled me with what she asked, for long I remember I tried to search for an answer but I failed to find it. It really made me think when she asked

"Mia didi, do fairies and angels exist?"

"Why?" I replied.

"Because I believe they do. Will you find them for me?"

I heaved a sigh and just said "I will try".

The same night I dreamt about my grandmother. I just saw her visage which was looking so vibrant and she had carried a smile on her face. She would always take me to such mystical world with her stories yet I never tried finding about the age old myth. I too was now in a quest to find them with Parul.

Ten

One day Sardar called all the workers and told us to stand in a row and began to give away gifts that was wrapped in a shimmery cover. I felt excited to unwrap and see what was inside. We had no clue about anything and why were we given without any occasion. I grew inquisitive. Perhaps Sardar too noticed gestures but he did not say anything and left the place. Then one of his sons apperared in the scene and gave away the news that it was Sardar's birthday tomorrow. Later when we all went back to our refuge after the work in the mansion was over I secretly went inside the bathroom to see what he had given. There was this beautiful salwar-kameez and I fitted perfectly in it, the pink colour made me look beautiful. We all had to report for work early tomorrow so while on bed I kept thinking about what the celebration would be like. But more than anything I was happy because tomorrow was my birthday too.

"Happy birthday" I whispered to myself the very next morning and wore the new set of clothes and all of us marched to wish Sardar the best of wishes with eager eyes. The mansion looked so appealing with the colourful festoons hanging here and there and then there were roses and marigolds whose smell lingered in the air. Sardar could be seen nowhere but only his two sons seemed to be busy. I had never imagined that I would be in a place like this which had always remained in my imaginations and in the stories of my grandmother. I knew she was watching over me from above. I smiled looking at the sky.

Soon the silence was broken by the hoard of people, all belonging to the highest ladder of the society. The party was one like a wedding with all the pomp and pleasure with guests grouping here and there. Some busy with the food and some with Sardar who had worn a handsome suit and had matched it with black coloured turban. Unfortunately, I had to be with the kids as they were not to attend the so called "adults party". However, all of us cuddled together in front of a big window and watched the crowd. The ladies were all sophisticated and from a distant I watched the two mothers of the kids who looked equally beautiful. Their mother-in-law had her own charm even in her grey hairs and wrinkled face.

"Didi, Can we all go and join them?" Parul asked me with much anticipation. She was the youngest among all the four.

"No dear, we cannot but we can watch them silently." I answered.

"Please didi." Nikhil began protesting.

"I too want to see dadu while he cuts his birthday cake". Nigam replied.

I remained silent as I had no answer for anyone because I was already warned beforehand that kids were not to join the party and I had to keep the close watch. Just then Kiran came up with an idea.

"Didi, why don't we play birthday party here in the attic? We will celebrate on our own."

"How is that possible?"

Then she brought some muffins from the tray that was on the table in the room and lighted a small candle onto it. I had to pretend that I was the Sardar and had to cut the cake. Soon all of them gathered around me and told me to be in the centre and started to hum the birthday song. I cut the cake which made me as emotional as it was actually my birthday. When the knife sliced the muffin a small drop of tear ran down my cheeks and touched it. Luckily nobody noticed much and we all ate together.

The party was the one like a dream that I had seen just in the movies as when I was a small kid, my parents would sit on the ground in rows to watch the cinema together, all rejoicing as the pockets would be warm and loaded after the monthly bonus. And back then I would also accompany them though after an hour I always reached in my dreamland because then I did not understand anything but the party scene would excite me like a young doe. It was already midnight the kids were already asleep and I felt myself like a high towered maiden witnessing the creation outside which then had been illuminating amidst the thousand lamps that slowly rose from below and made the sky look like a crown of diamonds.

My birthday had never been so special and for the first time I realised that I too was precious. For that one moment I was the queen of the world. The sky glowed and smiled at me. I closed my eyes and silently made a wish to God to direct me in my path and polish and make me gold. Suddenly I grew strong, wondered did God actually bestow his blessings on me. No pains and burdens that had been suppressed in my heart for long. I was a free bird though still under the captive but my soul was not chained and my spirit free from all the bondage.

After that day I was rewarded with one more thing and that was I had to no more live in that concrete building with others rather I began to stay at Sardar's mansion to look after the kids. It was way better than the place where I had to live before. I found my heaven in that small room which was now free from cobwebs and mosquitoes, no more foul stench. More than anything I could now sleep in peace with Mantu by my side, a new girl with the cleft lips. While I would be with the kids, she was assigned with the duty to be with the ladies of the house and to help them in their personal chores. After the day's laborious work often we would plunge in the bed and share the never ending tales about our previous lives. In the very short span of time we had grown closer to each other that if I would sit silently and not speak to her she would know that something is not right with me and in every way she cheered me until I would laugh till the tears would come out from my eyes and finally I had to stay "Now, will you stop?". She would dance by tuning the old radio without paying any heed to the songs and the beat. Her hands would swing in the air up and down and her feet tapped on the ground. She just danced even if the music was slow or rapid. For her my smile was most important. Sometimes she reminded me of Gayatri because in her I had found the same person and we began sharing the same bond of immense love and sisterhood.

Eleven

Life inside the mansion was totally different from the one that I had thought about when I had seen it for the first time. Back then, I was just hypnotised by its external beauty. The inner core had a story to tell. To my amazement, Sardar was married twice and her portrait hung proudly on the carved wall of his well furnished room which would always carry the aroma of something sweet. One day I hid myself from every one's eye and sneaked inside his room and then I was encountered with this mystery. A huge man perhaps Sardar in his youth grinned at me from the image in the front. He wore a bright coloured turban and some jewels around his neck and completed himself with a sword on his one hand that made him look no less than a maharaja of some ancient palace. He looked happy with the lady in red by his side from head to toe and bedecked with jewellery that made her look like a maharani. They both were in a complete bliss. The present woman and the one in the picture were like chalk and cheese. There was one more frame just below the portraiture where once again Sardar was there with his another wife.

Mantu and I were not allowed to cross the premises from our room, neither were we free to talk to the rest of the workers. All were given their own chores. We could barely communicate. Sometime we heard at night a woman lamenting, her cries would be so shrill that pierced our eardrums, frightened both of us and we would remain wide awake and took our ears close to the door and Mantu peeked from the small hole at the building where both the sons of Sardar were with their respective wives and children. Even the children would shout and beg for mercy when it would be difficult to calm a man's rage, how petrifying would be the scene we would always wonder. There was no peace within only when the children played, their fits of laughter echoed and just like the serene waves of the sea erode the remnants of the shore, and for once the mansion would effulge in joy and after sometime the same humdrum of the torturing silence rolled all in its dark cloak.

Sardar was a loner and all he did was bask all day outside lying flat on his armchair with his eyes closed and lost in his deep thoughts until someone jerked him from his slumber. He always kept a journal by his side and scribbled something and would stop if he caught me staring at him from the staircase where I would wait for the kids to finish their study hours with a private tutor on whom Mantu had a huge crush. The first time when she told me about her secret admire I remember how she had blushed profusely and since that day she always told me to keep tracks on him whenever he arrived. She made silly excuses just to catch a glimpse of his and when nobody would be there she walked back and forth the long corridor trying his extra large slippers. The tutor was young but elder to us; dark skinned and wore every time thick glasses which made him look like a big brother of a school going sister.

"Mantu, do you find him handsome?" I asked her one day.

"I do." She answered coyly.

Then she began to narrate her story without a stop. She said

"You know what happened today Meera?"

"What?"

"He bumped on me in the staircase. And later helped me to collect the broken pieces of the cups, the tea stained his shirt but he did not mind rather he apologised to me with kind looks and when the blood oozed out from my finger he safely took out the handkerchief and tied around my fingers."

"So, how are you feeling now?"

"Ecstatic. I am totally in love. I want to confess it to him."

"Are you serious?"

"Yes, please I need your help."

I remained silent because I was well aware about the consequences that would follow and how bad it will be. That it will be hard to face the truth about the denial because it was never possible, not even in dreams. But Mantu had now made up her mind that she will be conveying her feelings and she needed me. At that time I felt that life can be unpredictable. To her I was more than Meera, a sister like figure on whom she could always rely; the look that she had put on her face was so innocent that made it difficult for me to disappoint her. I chose to remain silent and not tell her that she in no way matched with the tutor. At last I replied in a very faint voice

"Okay."

The nightfall could not make me fall asleep. I laid still, my eyes raised up against the ceiling. I was in deep thought as to how I would help Mantu and make her long dreamt fantasy change into a reality which was like trying to move a mountain with a finger knowing already that it is never possible. The room was dark though not pitch dark as I could see my shadow in the adjacent wall and I remembered something, the hand movements that I would make to cheer my sisters when they would cry. I still knew to create a butterfly by joining the two thumbs side by side and then stretching the palms and moving them slightly just in a way the bird takes its flight.

"Meera are you not sleepy yet"? I heard Mantu asking me.

"Not yet". I answered.

"I had a dream Meera". She stated.

"What was the dream?" I asked.

"I cannot recall the entire picture but I saw myself feasting over a chicken flesh." She giggled.

"You are funny". I said.

"What are you thinking?" Mantu questioned.

"Nothing let us sleep". I answered.

I pulled the blanket and covered myself and inside I shed tears of loneliness and a fear for the unknown.

Twelve

The gleam of hope that flickered in Mantu's heart made her always plea for help before me. Never could she understand that how torturous it was and how much more difficult. I was absolutely not a fairy neither I had a wand that I could cast a spell and make her the princess and the tutor her prince. If I had the power at first I would vanish myself. Yet I tried each day to muster the courage and talk to him but I failed each time. At night like the defeated soldier I would lie still in bed until Mantu would break the silence by firing the bullets of questions and one or two would even pierce my heart.

One day I decided to write a note to the tutor and hand him over with the help of Kiran. She agreed and hence I told her to write

"Please meet me at the gate in the evening.

Meera".

By this time the tutor was well aware of my name as every day I would offer him a glass of water when he would come to teach. And one day he had asked my name in a very polite way.

"May I know your name Miss?"

"Meera". I had replied.

"Nice name". He had smirked at me".

The whole day I kept a close watch on Sardar and his entire family and the other servants around. Mantu knew everything and now wore a smile of complete satisfaction. I waited impatiently in the room for the class to get over. Everything was clear in my head as what I would do that I would confess Mantu's love for him with the girl by my side so that she could also witness the entire scene and later not curse me for the tutor's refusal. Soon I noticed the tutor coming out. After he had left Kiran gave me the assurance that she had given the note which I had told her to deliver.

"Did he say anything?" I inquired.

"No. He just slipped the note inside his pocket."

"Okay."

"What was inside the note didi?"

"Nothing, please do keep it as a secret." I smiled at her.

I was bewildered that whether the tutor would come or not. However, I hoped that he would and Mantu by my side, we marched forward by covering ourselves with shawls. Many things wandered around my head and we reached the decided point. There was no trace of him yet so we waited. It continued for sometime still he did not come. I could notice Mantu's smile fade away, then she started to sob. I did not want to comfort her but rather laugh at her foolishness as she did not want to believe what was so clear in front of her that he was long gone. Her innocence began to irritate me. I felt like to grab her arms and shake her to and fro and yell loudly at her so that she could break the castles of her air.

"Mantu, we should go now." I said.

"He will come". She replied.

"He will not, why not you understand."

"You betrayed me Meera." She cried out.

"I did not. I had given him the note." I protested.

"You are a liar." She commanded.

"Why would I do that to you?" I replied.

"Because he would surely come if he had found the note. He loves me. This is what you don't want to understand. You are jealous of me."

Mantu ran away in rage. Her hopes died out and perhaps her dream shattered but what could I do but stand and watch her go. At once I felt that by being truthful did I commit any sin? Back in the mansion I searched for her but could find her nowhere. After a while Kiran came up to me with a trembling voice.

"Meera didi, you are being called."

"Why?"

She did not speak any word further. I sensed that something was definitely wrong and when I came out I saw Mantu with Sardar with the same note which I had given to Kiran in the morning.

There were no tears in her eyes. Her eyes were fixed upon me and stared long with her bulging eyeballs. Sardar stood with no movement, one hand carrying the note and the other inside his pocket.

"What is this?" he asked, pointing towards now crumpled note.

I had no courage to look him in his eyes. My head started to turn dizzy. My anxiety rose up to the brim. I did not know what to say or how to frame the good explanation keeping Mantu on the safer side because I wanted to save her from the trap, from all the bitter consequences that would follow.

"Will you tell me the truth?" He further asked and gestured Kiran to go inside.

I did not utter a word and stood there with my head facing the ground. It was already dark.

"Mantu, I want you to speak for her." Sardar ordered.

"She is in love with the tutor. Even after being denied she tries always to woo him". She very easily put the false blame on me breaking the bond of an everlasting sisterhood. I closed my eyes and waited now for Sardar to speak as now I stood on the edge of the cliff and Mantu had already pushed me hard. My downfall made her victorious.

"Is that true?" Sardar asked me in stern voice.

I closed my eyes again. Tears rolled down my eyes and softly I replied "Yes". I had already fallen into a trap. There was no way out so I chose to remain there because If I would deny then I would be hated more for telling the truth because sometimes honesty is dangerous especially when you have already been chained by the false accusations.

"You will leave this mansion tomorrow." Sardar gave his verdict and left with the wrinkled note on the ground.

I stood in my place numb. I started to sob. I did not want to leave because I had no place to go in the big city as such where it was so easy to be lost in the crowd and when you are all by yourself with no safe refuge of your own, it was more vulnerable to be preyed on. But before I would leave I wanted to know that how did Sardar find the note.

Thirteen

"Meera didi, I swear I did not tell him." Kiran whispered in muffled voice. She had come to justify herself.

"I know that." I replied.

Mantu's presence in the room did not affect me. She sat in one corner ignoring my presence too. The silence was indeed torturous when at once her laughter would echo and seeing her so elated even after hard day I too would rejoice. Those moments now seem so distant like it never existed.

"It was the tutor, didi. He gave the note to Daadu." Kiran spoke again.

"Oh, is it?" I answered.

Mantu was still with no movement yet her ears were attentive and perhaps now she too was well aware of the truth that I never betrayed her.

"Yes didi." Please don't go. Kiran began to plead.

"I wish I could stay". I said with tears that welled up my eyes.

"You can stay". She replied in a voice that was so clearly highlighting the fact that how much she wanted me to stay. All I could do was look at her and force a smile on my face.

"Now you should leave." I urged her.

The whole night was spent in a complete silence neither Mantu spoke nor did I. She turned towards the wall showing her back and lay on the bed as if she was frozen for the night. Once again we had become the strangers like the very first day when she had entered the room with much nervousness. That night she was frozen like the way she was now and my words had choked in my throat as the way it is at the present moment. The pain within me was of a kind that could not make me cry but I was being poked hard inside. I was bleeding. The sign of the excessive blood was the way I had been sweating profusely. I tried to sleep yet I could not because now everything was coming before my eyes like a flashback just like the slides one after the other that moved in front of my closed eyes rapidly and suddenly I was fettered by those memories from where I wanted to escape, run away and find a solace in my heart. I was tired of being rejected every time.

Fourteen

I was dressed in ripped fishnets and ragged miniskirts and a thin blouse from above that only covered some part of my skin. The cosmetics lay in order with some lipsticks, puffs and powders, mascara and other basics. The room was cluttered. Clothes scattered. The small bulb flickered as if it was to die out soon and leave me in pitch darkness. My nails had grown long. They were painted red, cut uneven as time to time I chewed and spoil the shape. This is why they were brittle. My legs were crossed and moved them as if trembling due to chill. The bruise on my right thigh was paining, it had turned bluish green. A tiny room it was, walls scratched, the scraps of once freshly painted wall had come out. My bed was positioned near the small window from where only the drains could be seen rather smelled and the smell would be awful during the rainy season. I shared my room with none unlike others. I chose silence as my friend and the wandering thoughts that I would think when alone was my favourite pastime. My safe refuge was indeed that small den of mine in Lal Bazzar.

"Meera?" I heard someone call my name.

"Is it time?" I asked to Baridi.

"Baridi" was actually the shorter form for 'Bari- Didi' or elder sister. She was the eldest amongst all of us and with most profound experiences while we were amateurs.

"Yes. They have arrived." She answered by taking a brief glance at the mirror.

"How many are they?" I asked.

"Very few." She replied.

"I don't want to go". I begged with my both palms joined together.

"Oh, not again Mira. This is not your first time. You have done this before." She commanded by keeping both her hands at the side of her fat belly.

"I am scared."

"No one is going to hurt you darling. You will be fine."

"My bruise hurts still".

"You can bear. Be a strong woman."

"Please allow me to stay."

"Leave." She at last screamed and frightened me to death that I trembled, stood up and left the room only because I was a sex-worker now.

I was aware of it when I was first introduced to this place by this known person whom I had met in the nearest railway station soon after I left Sardar's mansion as according to his command. The whole night I spent in one corner with clothes and a little money that I had safely hidden in my bosom as my only possession. I spent half the time hunting for a common face amidst such a huge crowd in a hope to return back to the place where I belonged. I had been abandoned by all. I had become like a stray dog with no body to take the ownership. With a growling stomach I had been there lacking confidence to even stand and buy a bun or two. I felt as if somebody will grab me from behind and pull me to another pit from where it will be very difficult to come out.

My eyes opened in the crack of dawn when He had been standing before me perhaps from a minute long gazing as if I was from some other planet. I had been sleeping in that small odorous corner.

I sat erect and eyed back to the person as I was the feast to his eyes.

"Hello Miss". He spoke with a wide grin and lighted the cigarette.

I did not speak a word and stood up in order to fasten my pace and go somewhere else.

"Wait. We know each other." He said

"I don't know you". I replied with a stern voice.

"Your memory is so weak. Try to recall".

I observed him carefully. He was half bald. His face was covered with the stubble of several nights. His face was grim and oily. He wore a brown coloured shirt that was now crinkled and one grey coloured pant which he had teamed with a leather shoe. It had become very difficult for me to identify him.

"Who are you?" I asked.

"Oh Meera, you are still the same." He answered with disdain.

"Well, you be who you are then. I do not bother to know you." I replied with an agitated look.

"I am Raajan". He answered which took me in a complete state of utter astonishment.

"Are you serious?" I asked him and started to panic.

"Yes". He replied and took out a cigarette from his pocket.

"But you look so different."

"I am the same person whom you left a very long time ago."

"But what on earth are you doing here"? I further asked.

"Following you". He answered with the same disgusting grin.

I hated him for who he was and more than the hatred I was engulfed in wrath and with the each second that passed that fateful day I felt like choking him to death by pressing his throat.

"Anyway I will go now". I said. Though I had no clue about where I would be going.

"No, Wait." He commanded.

"I am going Raajan". I said with a curt voice.

"Where? You will easily be lost in this big city."

"I know where to go."

"Here, this is from Gayatri." He said and took out a brown packet from his backpack.

The moment I heard Gayatri's name I grew curious.

"What is that?"

"I don't know." He answered and handed me the packet.

There was an old photograph of mine and Gayatri that we had taken in our happier times on the garden. We both looked so joyful amidst the flowers. I realised that her memory had become blur but now I began to ruminate and wanted to know more about her whereabouts. But why was he carrying the picture anyway? Did he know that he would be meeting me?

"Do you know where she is?" I questioned hiding the tears that was brimming in my eyes.

"Yes, Of course I know". He replied with a great satisfaction as if this was what he wanted to hear from me.

I had million things to ask him about my family, Gayatri and himself. But I wanted to keep them aside until I meet my soul sister.

"Take me to her". I finally replied.

Fifteen

We reached a house at the end of the street. It was a secluded big apartment, well maintained and clean from outside with evenly cut hedges on the entrance and the whole building was painted in red. I paid more attention to the atmosphere around; no noise could be heard, mysterious and alienated from the outside world. There were no neighbouring houses but just a wide empty street that had melted my bones. I was exhausted that I just followed Raajan wherever he was taking me like a meek lamb that follows its shepherd.

A man entered the scene. He was perhaps in his middle age and stretched his hand from the other side of the long staircase and motioned in air. We followed him. On reaching the third floor, the man rang the bell. A fat woman who looked like a typical owner opened the door. She smiled at us, her teeth was stained red as she was munching the betel leaves and when the juice oozed out from the corner of her mouth, she wiped it with the edge of her sari. The lady then took out a pouch which she had hidden beneath her blouse and gave it to Raajan. Suddenly the woman came to me, held my wrist and began to pull me inside.

I jerked and tried to free myself and cried out loudly,

"Hey, where are you taking me?"

"Go with her, She will take you to Gayatri." Raajan answered.

"Will you not come?" I asked with my hand still under the woman's hard grip.

"No. I have to go now." Raajan answered.

And before I could speak anything, the woman with force pushed me inside the room and the door was shut. I began to panic and called out for help foolishly because there would come no help now. The room inside was colourful, the bright curtains that dangled down from the doors and windows were mystical. I had never seen such elaborated decor in any of the mansions where I had been before.

"Where is Gayatri?" I asked to the woman who was then lighting the cigarette.

"There is no Gayatri". She replied and blew the smoke on my face and I began to cough.

"What is this place?" I questioned her again.

"You will know it soon." She said.

"Get me out of this place. I no longer want to be here." I agitated.

She called her men. They grabbed me tight and threw me inside a room and locked it from out. I screamed and banged the door as many times as I could. Helpless, I mourned for death inside that vacant room which only had one bed and a small ventilation to let the outside light pass through.

Later, I felt a cold shiver in my body as I had been sleeping without my own notice for a long time on that cold dirty floor. I was thirsty, my mouth was dry. I went ahead and banged the door loudly. A man opened and called the same fat lady of the house.

"Yes?" she said.

"Water." I replied in a feeble tone.

I drank from the bottle like never before that I had been thirsty for ages.

"Where is Gayatri?" I asked her one more time in a hope that she will take me to her.

"Listen; there is nobody here whom you are looking for. You are a worker now, soon to be called a 'Sex-Worker'. We have paid for you to your Uncle Raajan. You belong to us now".

I was astounded for a moment in my place. I couldn't digest well the word 'Sex-Worker'. I started to beg her for mercy.

"Let me go please." I grabbed her feet and started to weep bitterly.

She kicked me aside and called the entire girls who were working under her. One by one they stood in front of us bedecked with accessories and scanty clothes.

"See Meera, look at them. They were all like you when they came here. You are not the only one." She tried to calm me down.

"I do not want to be here and sell my body to the innumerable men." I told her in anger.

"Enough. We will start our work from tomorrow. Get back to the rooms. And you stay here." She said by pointing her index finger at me.

"Follow me". She said.

She took me to the extreme end and showed me one small room.

"This is yours". She said.

I remained quiet.

"Don't dare to come out of this room ever only when I will call you or the consequences will be bitter." Her voice was very demanding.

I did not answer anything.

"You understand?" she asked.

I just nodded my head and went in.

Next day the fat lady called me and took me to one of the workers there who looked bit matured from the others. The woman had a bulging figure and her tight fitting shirt enhanced her breasts and made them extra large.

"We call her Bari didi". The owner said.

"Enroll her for tonight?" she asked.

"Yes. But she has to change her appearance first." The fat lady answered.

"I will do that." Bari didi replied.

I had no clue whatsoever. All I knew was that I was soon to be transformed. In a minute, I couldn't identify my own reflection in the mirror.

"You look perfect now". Baridi said.

It was not obviously perfect for me to be dressed in such skimpy clothes. I tried to adjust the skirt and pull it down to my knees. My thighs were bulging. As for my shirt, I was to unbutton it down to the place where the cleavage could be seen.

"Now go to the room". The fat lady commanded.

She whispered something in Baridi's ear and both bursted into laughter. Perhaps, I had been the topic of their joke.

I went to my room and closed the door. A man had been waiting for me in a corner with his eyes lit up. He was a young fellow.

I was nervous and perspiring.

In no time he pulled me towards him and I could do nothing.

I kept silent.

It was an awkward moment for me to come under the grip of an unknown man.

"Come I won't hurt you." He said.

"Who are you?" I asked.

"Your customer for tonight." He replied.

The very word 'customer' shook me from within.

I denied to the truth which I already knew that I had to let him touch me and exploit me without speaking a word.

The man rose up from his place. He held the collar of my shirt and hurled me on bed. I was filled with fear.

"What are you doing?" I asked.

"Don't speak a word else I will kill you." His anger had reached up to the brim.

Then he took out his belt and tied my legs on a wooden pole of the bed. I started to panic and screamed for help.

The entire night I was spanked for no reason. The man was ferocious and lunatic. He only tortured me. I was like a toy in his hand with which he could do whatever he wanted to as If I was lifeless. Nobody was there to hear my cry. I cursed my fate but was of no use. My skin burnt and I shrieked in pain when he poked the hot cigarette butt on my thighs and bottom. The pain was unbearable.

I could not understand my fault and God being so cruel and mean to me. Why every time I was fated for such brutality. That my life was a dark tale of sorrows and it was hard for the sunshine to penetrate in the thick vale of unfortunate clouds. I lay still till the morning half naked and weeping in pain. The man had already left.

"Meera, are you there?" I couldn't recognise the voice which was coming from outside.

She pushed the door that was half opened by the man and came inside. Horrified at the sight she was alarmed.

"Meera, Are you alright?"

I could only hear her voice and couldn't reply.

"Look at you". She said again.

I could feel her hand on my back. I jerked in pain.

"Sleep still." She whispered and on my bare back she applied something that was burning my skin.

"It will relieve your pain. Just ignore the burning sensation."

"Are you Baridi?" I murmured with my eyes closed.

"Hush Meera, don't speak."

It was her who had come to me.

"I knew you would be in trouble". She said.

"How did you know that?"

"My sixth sense maybe." She answered.

"It hurts. That man treated me brutally like I was just a lifeless log of wood."

"There is nothing anyone can do here even if you complain. Once you fall in this trap, it is hard to find a way out." She replied.

"I want to go home." I said.

"This is your home now. I have been here for past twenty years. I was as young as you when I came here. I underwent more fatal tortures."

"Why you never tried to run away?" I questioned her.

"Where would I go?"

"To where you belong, the place from where you came."

"I was sold to the brothel keeper by my father. Do you think they would ever accept me? He was a drunkard. Every day was a nightmare to see him abusing my mother and making her bear child after child. So I chose to stay here and face every situation even though if it was life threatening."

"I remembered my own family and that unfortunate day when Baba gave me to Raajan. My sisters and how would they be and how much they could have grown by now."

I closed my eyes and ruminated over the bygone days spent with Arpana and Gayatri. In some time I fell asleep later woke up by the loud beatings on the door to welcome some more men in my chamber.

There was no room for denial inside the brothel. We had to do what we would be ordered to do. Men from all walks of life would come and age was not a limit. At one such time I had to sleep with a sixty year old. I was half his age elder to my own father. However I couldn't deny his advances. It was so shameful yet it was the part of my work.

Sometimes I would just examine my body, how fast it had changed from what it was before to what it had become now. Nothing made sense and my prayers were still not answered. If all were equal before God then why would he shower ease and joy in the lives of few chosen ones and why so many shares of pain and sorrow in the lives of the unfortunates like me?

We were treated as heartless creatures and in a day we had to invite many men in our chambers who were again without kindness and would just come to seek the satisfaction. We were not handled with care at all by them. They were all animals in disguise and their acts beastly who showed no mercy but only they carried malice in them.

The brothel everyday welcomed many new girls and women and the ones who would be getting old were thrown out on the streets leaving them on their own. I could not imagine living such life and every day I tried to escape from the reality and in despair I would fantasise about a different life. There would be no brothel and no men. I hoped for a better future that a day will come when my sorrow will disappear. I will get a chance to live a life on my own terms. Will that day ever come? How many days was I to spent building the castles on air? Then I would just close my eyes.

My heart would be heavy, my eyes brimming with water. Hence it would be hard to hold myself back and I would cry aloud shedding vale of tears. When the tears would stop and I would feel light, once again I would get ready to satisfy men in my room.

Sixteen

My life had no meaning. It felt as if I was in the chasm struggling hard to come out but every time I tried my wings were cut. My body was not mine. It belonged to those men who would come to savour my taste, play with my existence.

I kept wondering about all this when somebody knocked hard on the door.

I opened and found myself startled. There had been no men around just us and all were rushing upstairs with blank expression.

"What is going on?" I asked one of them.

She did not answer me as she was equally ignorant as I was.

On reaching up, we saw Ruby hanging on the ceiling fan. I screamed in horror. Somebody closed my mouth from behind.

"There will be a police raid today so all hide in the basement." The pimp shouted on top of his voice that was standing beside the brothel lady.

"Hurry up". The lady said.

We don't know what happened with Ruby's body. Was it burned, disposed, buried or just thrown away in some pit? She was too young to commit such an act. Nobody knew the actual reason of her death but it was rumoured that she had been tortured brutally by the same customer for several days.

All of us began to walk towards the basement where we always hid ourselves unwillingly. There were secret chambers to hide. We all longed to escape from the shackle but our voices would hardly reach them. This way we had to stay inside the air tight compartments as long as the search would not be complete. A small hole would save us from staying alive from where the air would pass. The brothel owners never told us what reason they would make to conceal the ugly truth and luckily they were never caught till the present time.

We all kept mum inside. Nothing could be heard. In some time we came out but I decided to remain there. I did not mind the darkness neither the space. All I wanted was to stay alone.

"Come outside. What are you waiting for? They are all gone." Simi said.

"Yes. You go ahead." I replied.

When everybody left I came out and observed the room carefully. It was actually an armoury. Old things lay cluttered here and there. It was dirty and a foul stench lingered in the air. I had been here many a times before yet I had never had a close look of the room. I would always live in the same chaos with which I would enter but this time I chose to stay. Even though the room was a muddle but it was not dark except the chambers. The light had penetrated in the room so I decided to follow it. I went further and found finally what I had been searching for so long. There was one small door which was left open. On pushing it I discovered that it was the backyard of the building from where anyone could getaway. I stood in amazement and without giving a second thought I stepped out to the open area.

I ran for my life both in tears and smiles. I had never been so much free as I had been at that time. I did not know where the road would lead me but I kept moving and did not turn back even once. The railway station was somewhere near I remembered. I asked a lady for the direction at one time and I followed her instructions carefully. I had every possibility to get trapped again so I wanted to get inside the train as soon as I could and flee from the place which had made my life a living hell.

On reaching the station, the memories came before me in glimpses; that unfortunate day when I was caught by Rajan and taken to the place that had changed my life entirely. Had I not met him then perhaps my life would have been much better.

Nobody had time to stop and stare. All seemed busy with themselves and their own lives. And this is indeed what life is. All live for themselves and run to make a better living. And people like us; we are the savoury to their taste buds that when life knocks hard or is seeking for some pleasure we become so welcoming. At other times we have no identity.

I was thirsty and found a water tap nearby. I drank until I fully quenched my thirst and splashed some water on my face. I did not know where I was to go next yet I knew that I wanted to get away. I sat and stared to the trains that had halted for a while. There was buzz around of passengers, hawkers, beggars and above all the train timings were being announced. I woke up from my trance when a cold hand rested on my shoulder. Turning back I found out that it was an old lady asking for some penny. I was as helpless as her and had nothing to offer. I motioned a 'no' with my hand. S he pleaded more for some time. I did not respond and finally she left after getting affected by my adamant attitude.

The train sounded its alarm and a black smoke came out from the engine. People began to hurry. I too rose up from my place and without giving a second thought I entered inside. The train moved in a jiffy. I was amidst the unknown faces as started to look for a seat. It was apparent for people to notice my helplessness. With an empty hand I had boarded the train. I felt lost and nobody to help me. I decided to sit by the door accompanied by a foul stench. I covered my face with my hands and rested my head on my knees. The train had achieved a certain speed. I would fall asleep but again would wake up from the high pitch call of the vendors eager to sell their goods.

I did not know where I had reached but all I knew was that I was moving away to some place unknown to me. My stomach growled with hunger so I decided to beg for some food to the every passenger that I was to meet in the various compartments. I hunched my back so that people would show some pity on me and think that I had been affected by some disease. I went forward and extended my hand. A young girl dropped a five rupee coin on my hand and I was exulted. During the entire course I was mocked by some while many ignored my call. However I collected few pennies that could buy me something to eat.

Tired I went back to the same place where I was earlier but this time there were few men too. I sat in the corner and waited impatiently for the vendor to come. After a while I bought a cup of tea and biscuits. It did not satisfy me entirely but it surely silenced my increasing hunger. It was already night and the train was still moving. The men began to smoke. They were playing cards with fits of laughter. The smoke choked me and I started coughing. However, none of them noticed me. After a while one of the men came with a handkerchief and told me to sniff it. I denied but he started to insist. I took it hesitatingly and covered from my nose.

In no time I started to feel nauseous. I could not do anything as I felt that I had been intoxicated. I wanted to scream for help but all I did was held my head to stop myself from falling down. My body was losing its strength.

"Are you fine?" I heard someone say.

"No". I replied in a faint and feeble voice.

"Who is with you?" he asked again.

"She is our sister. We will take care of her." another voice interrupted from somewhere

Seventeen

"Where am I?" I asked when I first opened my eyes. I did not know where I was and what had happened to me. I was in a journey on a train but now I was somewhere else. My heart was beating faster. I was totally in fear. My throat had dried and I was feeling bitter inside my mouth. I was lying on a bed in an empty room. The smell was of the medicine in the air. I growled with hunger. I was wearing the same clothes that I had been wearing. I turned towards the right and I saw a tumbler. I stretched myself to reach it but I could not. I heaved in pain.

A woman clad in white from head to toe entered the room. She found me awake and said

"Oh, you woke up?"

I was in utter confusion of what was going around me.

"What is this place?" I said.

"This is called a hospital." He replied.

"But why would I be in a hospital? What had happened to me?"

"Shall I call your husband? He will answer to all your queries."

"A husband?" I was startled.

"Yes. He brought you here and said that he wanted to sell your kidney to deal with your child's nearing death." The woman answered.

I shouted in horror when I heard about the loss of my kidney. I felt my lower abdomen and discovered that I was suffering with the pain due to this. The scar was prominent.

"This is a lie. I don't have a husband or a child." I cried out.

The other man entered the room and looked at me. The doctor had already left. I began to perspire in fear and the world revolved around.

He was the same person whom I had seen in the train along with his friends. The help that he had offered me by giving me the handkerchief was a well made plan. I had been abducted by them. As I had sniffed the handkerchief I had been unconscious.

"Who are you?" I shouted at him with an agitated look on my face.

"Your husband". He replied with a wry smile.

I felt like hurling the tumbler on his face. I was disgusted to hear him lying so direct to my face.

I stretched my mouth wide and closed my eyes to shout for help but in no time the man's broad palm reached my mouth and he took out a dagger and aimed on my neck. He held my hands together.

"Look girl, do as I say or you are sure to die." He whispered on my ears.

I was nearly choked and nodded my head to free myself from his hard grip.

"Why are you doing this?" I started to sob.

"It is none of your concern. Just obey to what I say." He said and hid the dagger inside his shirt pocket.

I was oblivious to everything. My fate was in the man's hand. He had the free will to decide as to where he was to lead me and in which direction I was to go.

"You will come with me in sometime". He commanded.

The man left the room and I lied on the bed feeling my cut. I felt handicapped without the kidney.

Soon the nurse came along with the doctor who checked my eye as if the pain would be seen in my pupils.

"How are you feeling?" He asked me.

I answered a forced 'fine'.

"You are ready to leave now." He said.

I managed to get up from bed with the help of a nurse.

"You are really a brave woman." She said.

I did not answer but went inside the washroom. I saw myself in the mirror. I looked pathetic. My eyes had the dark circles. I was pale and weak. I washed my face and cried covering my mouth so that nobody could hear. The scar ached while I cried.

I went out and saw the man waiting for me.

"Are you ready?" He asked.

"Yes". I replied.

A van stood in a distant. There were other people too. As I neared the vehicle I saw some more girls like me. I was startled.

"Get in quickly". The man said.

I did not ask him anything but obeyed to what he was telling me to do. My life was at a great risk.

On entering the van I figured there were altogether five girls and including me it would be six. The man took the driver's seat while his other companion sat next to him. All six of us huddled together.

The man drove us through the alleys and gutters and the dingy and dimmed colonies. None of us spoke to each other. All were in trance as if hypnotised by some spell unless mine was broken by the loud noise of a horn. The van had stopped in front of the brick house; half constructed and not painted at all.

"I feel sick. "The girl with a freckled skin said. It was loud enough for the man to hear.

"You will be alright once you enter the house." He said and got down from the van.

"What place is this?" I asked.

"Stay here unless I call you." He replied ignoring to what I had asked him.

He left us behind in the car with his friend to watch over us. We all kept quiet. I looked towards the girls with blank expression. They all looked tired. I wanted to start the conversation to break the torturous silence amidst us. We would look at one another but again turn our heads. Nobody smiled even.

"Come out now." The man shouted from the brick house.

His companion got down from the van and opened the door. One more time we all looked at one another perhaps searching on each other's face for the answer as to where we were being taken. We went towards the house with the man and on reaching the door my heart began to beat fast.

"You go first." The girl with the freckled skin pushed me.

I stood stiff speechless.

"We all will move together." I finally replied.

The man was leading us while his friend went back inside the van. The door was opened wide and we stepped into the unknown. On entering, we discovered that it was a large open hall and there were staircases. It was not as silent as it looked from outside. There was much hustle-bustle around.

"Where have you brought us?" I asked.

"To a brothel." He replied boldly.

"Not again". I whispered to myself.

One of the girls began to cry and yelled at the man.

"You cheated on me." She said.

The man kept quiet.

"Take me back home." She cried again.

She sat down on the floor and began protesting.

The man in rage grabbed her hand tight and dragged her from the floor. She cried more loudly this time.

We were terrified yet could not help her.

"What noise is this?" A lady appeared on the scene.

The man coughed. He looked towards the girl and she stood up and lowered her face.

"Here they are." He said.

The woman raised her left eyebrow.

"You may leave now." She urged to the man.

"My reward?" He replied.

Taking out a hefty note from her blouse she began to count.

"Here you go." She said and gave away the amount.

The man now satisfied returned without even giving a glance at us. I knew that we had been sold to the lady. We were her puppets now. I had already been to a brothel earlier which had torn me apart from within.

She took us upstairs. We saw tiny compartments where each of us had to spend the rest of our days in the brothel. I felt like a bird in the prison. I was free but now I had been captured again.

"You will live here in my command." The lady said.

I stepped in to my cell. There was a bed and some clothes scattered on the floor. I recalled to everything what the lady had instructed while climbing up the stairs. We were to pay her some amount from whatever we would earn from the customers. Only the food would be given to us and all other things we were to buy. The more the customers the better it would be for us.

I looked down from the window. It was an empty street but the lady had said that on the working days it would be busy. We were to lure the customers by signalling them from the window.

I lied flat on my bed. The cut still ached. I remembered my family, the various events that had taken place in such a short period of time. I thought about Gayatri, Arpana and Mantu with whom I had another set of memories. The twice attempt of mine to run away and every time I was cheated by some rogue and pushed in to the pit of flesh trade. As I ruminated on my past encounters, the several men with whom I slept it was nothing more than a nightmare to me. However, once again I was to live in the same nightmares and this time it could be even more ghastly I thought.

Eighteen

After a couple of days when we were given ample time to rest, Saheli appeared in my room with a long list of instructions written in her mind.

The same woman whom we had encountered on the first day. She was a lean woman with a bulging pair of eyes. She had only one arm and this is why she always covered herself with a shawl to hide her defect in her body.

"How is your cut now? Does it still ache?" She asked at first.

"No, not much." I replied adjusting the sleeve of my vest.

"Tonight. Your work starts from tonight." She said in an affirming tone.

I just nodded my head and gave her a look of acceptance.

"So get ready by 10. You all will be taken shortly."

"By whom?" I questioned.

"You must look very appealing with no dearth of fear and shyness on your face. You also are to be submissive, quiet and dainty." She replied ignoring to what I had actually asked her.

"Where will I be taken?" I asked again.

She just looked at me widening her eyes as if I was to read the answer on her eyeballs. She then tapped me on my shoulder and left the room. I stood for a moment clueless and anticipating about what would happen to me. Before me was the time which now was running short. I prepared to face the trial with a heavy heart. I remembered that day when I had waited for my customer and offered myself like some kind of bait to him. And in the end all I had received were bruises all over my body. I silently prayed to God that this time I may not have to face the same consequences. While I was dressing up I figured that I had been put to a different category. I did not had to attract customers from the window as according to what the brothel lady had said to us on our very first day. I was getting ready to go somewhere alone or in a group I was yet to find it out.

"Are you done?" I heard a voice from outside.

"Yes". I replied.

"Hurry up. It is almost time." She confirmed.

I opened the door. The lady had left already. I went downstairs and found the other girls too. I was happy that I was not alone. All were dressed for the night in scanty clothes. We were four of us. I did not see the girls who had come with me the other day. There were new faces before me. We stood and waited for Saheli.

"Where are we going?" I asked to the girl beside me.

"The Silver Oaks." She replied stressing much on the last letter's'.

"What is that?" I interrogated again.

"A hotel and a bar." She answered facing front.

Saheli arrived the very moment. Her heels made a rhythmic sound on the floor.

"Ladies for tonight." She said and pointed towards us to the man.

The man was to take us to the hotel. He looked at me and smiled. I showed no interest. We all headed towards the car that had been waiting for us outside. But before we entered the man stopped us.

"You all are hired by the special clients so do treat them well. I will see all of you in the morning and will bring back here." He said.

"Who are they?" Rinku asked.

I knew her name when she introduced herself to me a moment ago.

"Elite people." He replied with sparkling eyes.

I grew nervous as I thought about them and how would they be. We all got inside. The car moved in the pitch dark. Saheli waved us goodbye. After travelling for about half an hour we reached in front of a Porsche hotel. It was a tall building, multi-storeyed with large glass windows. On the entrance two young gentlemen stood erect and welcomed the visitors by opening the door for all who passed by.

"Don't come out of the car unless I give you a sign. Let me go first." The man suggested.

He got down from the car and went inside the hotel. We all began talking amongst ourselves.

"Yes I am from Bangladesh and was sold to the brothel since I was a thirteen years old." Maya told to all of us as we listened to her with rapt attention.

"So you have been working since that early age?" I asked her.

"Yes." She replied boldly.

"What is your story?" Rinku asked me.

I hesitated at first. They kept on insisting me. At last I shared them about my journey so far to the world of flesh trade. I narrated how I was given away by my own father to the man who had been aiming on my virginity for a long time. He exploited me and let me to be exploited by the other men too.

"I was born to a sex worker." Sapna said.

We all looked at her in amazement. She noticed our expression but did not react to it. Perhaps she had been used to it.

"What happened to your mother?" I asked again with much curiosity.

"Ladies, it is time now to go". We heard the man calling us from the back of the car where he was lighting the cigarette.

I hated him for interrupting. We all got down from the car without Sapna answering to my question.

"I will tell you later." She whispered in my ear.

The man inhaled the smoke taking a long breath and released the smoke from his mouth by opening it wide.

"Here are your keys". The man handed over the keys of our respective rooms.

We took them from his hand.

"Open the door, get in and wait for your client to arrive." The man spoke and stamped on the butt of the cigarette with the tip of his shoe.

We heard his command but did not answer anything. I had 'Room number 109' written on my key. I grew nervous. We all went together inside. We were already been told by the man that our rooms would be on the first floor of the hotel. As we all split into the different directions my heart was beating faster. The only thought that was running in my mind was about the man that how would he be. I unlocked the door. It was a big room, sophisticated with impressive interiors.

My client could arrive anytime so I checked myself in the mirror. I looked thin in the body hugging dress but my thighs were bulging. The mole on the side of my neck could be seen along with the cleavage. I was wearing the off shoulder dress. I felt something sticky beneath my feet. A chewing gum had stuck on the heel of my sandal. I took it out with the help of a tissue paper. Just then my stomach started to ache. I could not move suddenly. I screamed in pain and looked around for a glass of water. Somehow I crawled and reached for the water on the table near the bed. I stretched myself and my hand began to tremble. I took a sip. The pain increased more. I lied on the floor pressing my stomach with my both hands. It was actually the cut that was giving me the bitter pain. After a while I was again normal.

The cut ached no more. I had forgotten about the man who would be coming in my room. Hurriedly I got up, looked at the watch dusting the dust off my dress. It was midnight. This time I sat on the bed and patiently waited for my client to arrive. Sometimes playing with my hair and dangling my feet from the bed. I had kept the door half open.

After a while when he still did not come I went to the washroom and washed my face. I dabbed the towel on my face. I heard a noise outside; the sound was that of footsteps. When I opened the door I found a man sitting still on the chair. He looked very official. He was dressed in formals, white shirt paired with black coloured pant and tie with black and white stripes. He had taken off his coat. I assumed he would be in his mid forties. His hair had thin shades of grey and few wrinkles could be seen in his otherwise handsome face.

"Here you are." He looked at me exultantly.

I tried to hide my nervousness and controlled myself that I don't fidget. I chose to remain silent.

"What is your name?" He asked me in complete ease.

"Meera". I answered looking at him.

"You know who I am?" he tried to act superior.

I was clueless. But looking at his appearance I could at least assume that he could belong to the high class ladder. There was every possibility that he could also be the heir of some company. He was indeed a rich man.

I replied a confirmed "No".

"I am a lawyer. You know what does that mean?" He said signalling with his one hand to sit on the bed.

I did not know the exact way to define. I thought for a while and replied to him.

"You try to safeguard the laws of the country."

"Almost there. You are a very smart girl."

I felt happy from within not only that I was being able to answer smartly to what he had asked me but also that I felt safe with a total stranger for the first time in all this time. But why would he want to be with someone like me? What turned his mind to seek pleasure in a sex-worker when he could get many girls for free? I tried to seek for answers in my mind.

"What are you thinking?" He broke the silence.

"Why are you here?" I asked him fearlessly.

"The same thought is running within me that why am I here and for what purpose. I am a married man with two young sons. What will happen if they find out that their father is with a girl in a hotel room? How bad example will I set." He replied.

"When everything is so apparent before you then still you chose to spend your night with me?" I grew more confused.

He looked at me intently for some time. He took a deep breath as if he was trying to lessen the burden of grief that he was carrying within.

"I am detected with a disease, HIV positive. I am dying from within. And the worst of all I have to hide this from my wife and sons."

I had heard about the virus many times in the brothel. Since the brothel keepers would abandon anybody who would be found suffering from it. I was taken aback with what the man had just confessed before me.

"How did it happen?" I asked.

"I had sex with one of my colleagues. It was so sudden that after the incident she left her work and never contacted me again neither did I. But I was left with the scar of guilt for lifetime. I cheated on my wife who trusts me more than anyone. I call it a punishment from God that he is taking me away from her for her own good. I was transmitted with the disease from the lady."

I could well understand his pain.

"But the disease will change you physically. How will you cope with that? Your wife will detect it." I said.

"Before that happens I will take my own life." He replied with eyes brimming with tears.

I was deeply emotional. I did not know how to take control of the situation. I prayed silently for a healing to his tormented soul. I took his hand and made him sit with me on bed. He came near me. I told him to lie down, he did. I took his head and made it rest on my lap and started to stroke his cheeks and caress his hair. He closed his eyes.

"Do you feel good?" I asked.

"I am so much relieved." He replied.

I continued stroking him. I watched him sleep. The night had ripened and in that abysmal silence nothing could be heard except his breath. When he had finally slept I slowly shifted his head to a pillow and took off his shoes. I lied next to him. I faced him and kept my hand on his cheek. He was warm and asleep. I cleared the myth that I was the only victim of sorrow. All receive their equal share of suffering be it as a sex-worker or as a lawyer.

I closed my eyes. I was in perfect peace. I remained untouched. All men perhaps are not the same. But it is hard to come across one when all the time you are treated as nothing but a toy who works once it is paid and you can do anything with it, get down to any extreme level only to fulfil that desire of sexual pleasure. I yawned covering my mouth. I hoped that I did not wake up the person who was sleeping next to me. The man slept as if he had been sleepy for ages and tonight he finally met with that golden moment where he could unload the burden that he had been carrying. Sleep was now his solace. I wished that the sleep will transform him and he will no more feel the same feeling of languor.

Nineteen

I looked around but he was gone. As I woke up I could just find the room empty, only me inside. I was still groggy. I looked at the clock. It was 6 am. I had slept in a complete bliss. I tried to manage the wrinkled bed sheet and make it crisp ironed as it was before. I kept the pillow back in its position. There was a note on the table yet I could not read what was written. I folded it and slid inside my bra along with a thousand rupee note which the man had left me. I wished he would not have left so early that at least I could kiss him goodbye on his hand.

The phone rang. I hesitated at first to respond but I grew eager when it continued ringing till I picked it up. Before I could speak the male voice commanded.

"Slowly get down and go towards the right side of the hotel where the car was parked last night. Get inside the car. I will keep an eye on you."

It was the same person who had brought us here. I tied my hair into a ponytail. I wiped my smudged eyes with the help of a handkerchief. I looked fine. As I stepped out I did exactly what was being told over the phone. I lingered my eyes around, the girls were not there. The car was parked safely. As I neared it I saw all were inside, the three of them. The man came after I got in and immediately drove us past the hotel. The weather was nice but soon we would be locked up again in the tiny stuffy cells of ours.

Rinku's eyes were glued outside the window of the car. The other two sat quiet like me as all of us were in a trance yet to come out of the last night's hangover. I thought about the man and where would he be at the present moment. He was already dead just left with his living body, though he breathed but would count how many more breaths to breathe. The gun was already aimed on him just he was waiting for the right moment to pull the trigger. I felt pity on him.

THE WINTER

I was cold lying on the floor and panting profusely in pain asking God to have mercy on me. The room was dark with a window. I wanted more air on my lungs. I was choking yet I could not get up and open the window wide. The baby could come out any moment. I bit my hand hard to take control of the agonising situation. I cried out at last unable to hold back what was making me suffer so much.

I only heard the loud thud and someone broke inside the room before I lost my senses, my eyes closed and everything was dark. What had happened then I do not know but when I woke up I was lying on the bed. My belly was now flat as if the tyre had been punctured after many months. I was not alone in the room. I saw the brothel keeper and Rinku was with her. I suddenly remembered that I had just given birth to my baby. I had it inside me and now it seemed to be nowhere. I panicked to see it.

"Where is my baby?" I asked in a shrill tone.

Rinku and the brothel keeper had been talking to a man in spectacles. I assumed he was the doctor and he was as he approached me and said not to worry and my baby is safe.

"What is it? A boy or a girl?" I grew more curious.

"She is a girl." Rinku said and smiled at me.

I shed the tears of happiness. They brought the baby to me. I held her in my arms. Her eyes were closed. I kissed her delicate hands and forehead. I did not feel like shifting my gaze anywhere but just wished to look at her and cradle her in my arms for eternity. I kissed her again and she moved a bit. She made me forget every pain that I had suffered with earlier. It was a feeling of motherhood perhaps and now I was suddenly rejuvenated from my older self. For her I was ready to do anything, her happiness now meant more to me. I wanted to be the best mother in the entire world. She was my world now.

Rinku took her away and told me to get some rest. I refused to let her go.

"She is yours now. I am just taking her away for a while." Rinku said.

I tried to get some sleep but I couldn't. As I closed my eyes the nightmare returned again but in short glances just like I was watching slide after slide. I drank some water and lied down again counting the ceiling above me.

After my encounter with the lawyer on that fortunate night in a hotel room I was taken out as a hired sex-worker more often. I met with a host of men of all sorts. Some would treat me well while some would not. There were times when I was beaten and I would come back to the brothel with bruises. I had stopped crying. Tears had no role when a man would be in a fit of rage and animosity neither did I plea before them to not torture. I did whatever they told me to do.

One day a man asked me in the middle of the activity that how do I feel about my body when so many men have touched it in their own way. I thought for a while to answer him right because he had raised a thought provoking question.

"When I was a kid I thought only my grandmother had the right to touch me while she would give me bath. As I grew up I changed and began to think that I am the sole master of my body. I became more mature and realised that God has chosen a partner for each one of us who is called a spouse and has given the right to touch. But very soon I suffered a great upheaval in the way I thought because I was destined to be touched by many." I replied.

"How do you feel about your body?" He asked me again feigning unsatisfied attitude with what I had answered to him.

"I don't feel anything. I am numb to whatever happens with me. I stand in front of the mirror I see two facets of my own self. You are with one at the present moment and the other one dwells in me." I said.

"How are they different from one another?" He questioned me raising both his eyebrows.

"I am wearing a mask now of a sex-worker who has come to you to give you pleasure. When I go back I take that mask off. I become docile and naive as a doe. My heart becomes fragile, it breaks and I cry to collect the broken pieces so that tomorrow I wear the mask again with a strong heart."

After that day I felt I was more than just a sex-worker. My dreams were also valid. I dreamt of luxuriating in a bungalow. Even if it was too flamboyant for me I still could think that one day I would be free as a bird sheltering in a safe refuge.

The fear that I would carry earlier slowly started to disappear. I began facing men not as an amateur but I had become skilled. Sex is also an art indeed. One needs to know the correct way to seduce a man at first so that he is hypnotised. We have to welcome him in our secret chamber of pleasure which he comes seeking for. Slowly the art needs more attention because a man is not in the same mood always. We thus have to play various roles in this process of what we call sex. Agony was like another name for my life. I had to live with it every moment but never did I fall. It strengthened me more and more for my future.

And it so happened that one day I collapsed on the floor while Rinku was in my room trying to read the note which the lawyer had left for me. I was standing before the mirror while she sat on my bed. Her stammering voice however was making no sense. She was trying harder.

"Hey, I know the first word and the second too." She cried out in excitement.

I was already feeling nauseous when she was pondering over that paper for a minute long. She could not hear my silent plea for help. And I fell down perhaps with a soft thud. This is why Rinku only saw me when she was successful to identify the written two words. I was blacked out totally.

"Are you fine?" She asked me later with an honest concern.

I just nodded my head. I was not fine rather felt weak. I was lying on my bed. Rinku had to leave me because if we were caught together then we were sure to invite trouble. We were not to enter each other's room. This was one of the rules that were read to us in our own very first days.

"I shall go now. You take care. Will you?" she said.

I did not want her to leave perhaps because I felt her as my own. We were like sisters. She would remind me of all whom I had left behind with nothing more than their memories. Rinku left in a while with a funny whisper that made me smile.

I felt an uncontrollable urge to cry. I bursted out in tears seeping through my shirt. I changed my position and turned towards right. Tears were accompanied by hiccups. I knew I was soon to change from what I was. Would the change be good or bad? I left it to my destiny to decide. After all we are the mere puppets. I watched the palm of my hand close. There were lines all criss-crossed and I thought where I would be at the present moment. In which line would I be walking? My grandmother would often say gasping:

"Do not show your palm to anybody. They will change your destiny."

I would later give it a close thought. That was nothing but an age old superstition which my Grandma was fond of using it. But wasn't I becoming superstitious now? Time indeed changes everything.

As soon as I had collapsed that day I grew weaker. The morning sickness was constant and often I would wake up with a heavy head. I escaped from my work for two days when they found me genuinely sick. But I well knew that I was being recorded in the mind of the brothel keeper as the girl who has not being working for two days. That was indeed a serious issue. I had some money saved though. I could throw that on his face anytime if he would argue for my disability at the present moment.

"But you look fine". Saheli came up to me this time.

I was still lying on the bed when I was supposed to work. I had puked the earlier night. My head was about to burst with pain.

"Please take me to the doctor." I requested.

She looked at me for a while and thankfully agreed to my request.

"Get dressed up." She commanded and closed the door shut as she left.

I waited for her downstairs. She came with the same noise of her high heels. Her clothing reminded me of some party goer. She straightened her dress and wiped the corner of her eyes.

"I look fine." She said to herself and kept the handy mirror in her purse.

Twenty

The doctor looked at me with sympathetic eyes after he had scanned me internally. He was old. Did he know that I was a sex-worker? We perhaps had played our parts well. Saheli had made me her younger sister. Sometime she would pat my back and answered to almost every question that the doctor had asked me. I had never seen her that way before. At once seeing her speak so frequent the doctor had to stop her in between and he let me to voice out what I was going through.

I wished to reveal my real identity. Had Saheli not been there with me, I would have narrated him my entire story. But she was there carefully noticing me with a malicious heart. I had to hold myself back and I did so though hesitatingly.

"I feel sick and my head is heavy every morning." I had replied to him before he took me inside the veiled room and checked me thoroughly. When he put the stethoscope on my chest, the fear wrapped me around again. Will he strip off my shirt too? I thought but he did not rather treat me with much kindness.

And now he was in some deep thought. Saheli was terrified. She showed her fret by shaking her leg beneath the doctor's table. They had secretly conversed for a while. But why was I not allowed to listen to them? Was I going to die? I was impatient to know the matter.

The doctor cleared his throat and scratched his bald head. He would tell me now.

"You are pregnant." He blurted out the words and gave me the greatest shock of my life till then. How was I supposed to react, I did not know. I carried mixed feelings.

"How is that possible?" I swallowed the last words.

I was not supposed to ask that question though rather it had to be when it happened. Perhaps the same question ran on Saheli's mind too. Did she want to punish me? I ignored such thought.

"You have just conceived. The weakness and headache were the symptoms." The doctor said.

Tiny droplets of tears started to roll down my cheeks. I was overwhelmed with both happiness and fear. I tried to see Saheli from the corner of my eyes. She was gaping at me. I refused to say anything.

"I am prescribing you some medicines. You have to take proper care of yourself now." The doctor told.

I was anticipating about the consequences that were to follow after we leave from the hospital. What would she say about my pregnancy? Will she still push me to work? How would she explain to the brothel keeper?"

The doctor scribbled something in a sheet of paper. His handwriting made the writing worse to understand.

"Here you go." He gave the sheet to what he called a prescription to Saheli.

I had thought that Saheli would refrain from buying me the suggested medications. But to my surprise she bought without speaking a word to me. She no longer admired herself in the mirror in short intervals which she had done before. Now her gaze was just fixed in one direction.

But one thing that was making me feel secured was the medicines. Did Saheli want the baby too? If yes then why would it be? But again if she was delighted with the news then she would definitely talk to me. Here she was meditating silently over something with her eyes both open.

Later that night I was immersed in a whirlwind of emotion. I was battling with myself inside. I was tortured by Saheli's silence. It is indeed the best way to answer when words lose their power. We can interpret silence in many ways. It could be either positive or negative. But how was I supposed to coin a meaning out of it.

I had another life slumbering inside me. I would give birth to it in due course of time. And so I started to imagine. I was to be a mother but to a fatherless child. Unfortunately I would never be able to satiate the hunger of my child to know its father. I too was oblivious about it.

"What is it?" I had asked Baridi quizzically when she had showed me a small packet. It contained a rubber like substance.

That was the first time I knew about a substance called 'condom'. I had felt weird at first as I touched it.

"It is a very important thing to use while you have sex with men." She had told me. I had given her a confusing look and I did not had to reply her to her any further.

"The men wear it in their penis. It saves you from getting pregnant and protecting yourself from sexually transmitted diseases." She advised me.

However there were times when I had not taken her words so seriously and had slept without its use. This was why I had to face this day of being identified as a pregnant girl. But with the idea of pregnancy I effulged with joy too. The baby would be the reason to survive in this world which had otherwise treated me so harshly. The fear followed again for I was uncertain about its future. The brothel keepers were already so furious with me. And now I was growing a baby inside me that was indeed the terrible mishap that could happen in any brothel especially to a young worker like me.

What turn would my destiny take now? I had always been a destiny's child in anyway. I could never go in the planned direction. Whatever had happened to me till now it was definitely the handiwork of my destiny? I had not chosen to live my life this way as a sex worker. Never did I dream even in my wildest dreams. I was forced in it.

The next day the brothel keeper called me. I was ready for his wrath that was soon to crush me. As I opened the door I saw Saheli sitting in one corner with her hand covered as usual. The brothel keeper had two wives about whom I had heard before. I saw their faces for the first time. One was bulky while the other one was thin.

"What a contrast?" I had thought in my mind.

They closed the door as I stepped inside the room where the curtains were pulled blocking the lights from the outside sun. The brothel keeper then motioned me to sit on the chair while all of them stood around in a semi circle. I was clueless that what they were ought to do to me. I was more than terrified that I could not even look into the eyes of any body. Not even Saheli who had accompanied me to the hospital.

"Speak now. How did it happen?" The fat woman screamed at me.

"I don't know." I replied.

The brothel keeper then slapped my face. His hard hand perhaps left a mark on my skin. I touched my cheek. It burned.

"She has no room in this brothel anymore. She must leave." The brothel keeper shouted on top of his voice.

I continued lowering my eyes down. Seeing this the other woman grabbed my face with her hand and tried to pull it up. At that moment I remembered about Sapna. She had told me that she was born to a sex worker. What might have happened to her mother? I grew curious. Did she go through the same torture like me? I wanted to find her. I wanted to ask her only if I could escape.

All of them began to insist that I must leave the brothel. They could not bear my expense for such a long period of time. I looked at Saheli with hope but she too denied me to help.

"Please let me stay." I said.

I began to cry to gain some mercy. But all they did was torture me more as they pushed me on the ground.

"Where will I go in this condition?" I pleaded before them.

"This is the outcome of your own sinful deeds." Saheli spoke this time.

"You must abort the baby if you want to stay here." The brothel keeper came forward with an option. Hearing which my heart was deeply wounded.

"I will never do that." I protested.

How could I kill my own baby when just the other night I had been dreaming about it? I did not know which decision would favour me. However I was sure of one thing that I was never going to abandon my child no matter how hard it may be for me. I remained firm to what I had said. I would not change my mind.

"Will you agree if I will allow you to stay here and give birth to the baby but on one condition?" Saheli questioned me promptly.

I was joyous after hearing to what she had said. The brothel keeper and his wives were amazed at her.

"What are you saying?" All of them spoke in chorus.

"I am speaking sense." She replied.

Was I dreaming? I did not know. It did not look real at all to me. I did not bother about any condition that she would put before me. I was filled with euphoria only because I could give birth to my baby.

"Go for now. You will know it soon." Saheli ordered.

And I left the room with a swollen face and a happy heart.

There was a long conversation after that and nobody was to intrude in between. I knew this because I had stood there trying to eavesdrop. When nobody came out for some time I thought that it could be a fair chance now to meet Sapna and hear the rest of the story about her mother.

I watched my steps and carefully sneaked inside her room. It was an off day in the brothel so she was not with the customer. As soon as she saw me she was surprised and quickly bolted the door.

"What is going on? Is everything okay?" She asked me.

I took a deep breath.

"Yes it is. I came here to find something."

"And what is that?"

"I want to know what happened to your mother."

She began to laugh.

"Oh Meera, you are so silly. Are you still on the same hangover?"

I ignored her sarcasm.

"I may sound silly but I really want to know about your mother."

This time she was serious and looked outside from her window as if she was remembering what had happened in the past.

"My mother was murdered soon after I was born." She replied.

I was puzzled for a moment.

"How do you know that?" I asked.

"The brothel keeper is my half brother. We had the same father. He died after my mother's death." She replied.

Everything appeared to me so baffling. I tried to dig deep the inner secret about the brothel which had been hidden beneath for so long.

"I know what I am telling you are making no sense. But just sit patiently as I narrate her story." She said.

"My mother was sold from Nepal by her own cousins. She was very poor and illiterate. She thought she could earn some money and look after her ailing mother. But never had she known that she had fallen in the pit of hell until she was forced to sleep with men. She was described to be very beautiful that could melt anybody's heart. The brothel keeper who already had a son from his wife came seeking pleasure to her. She was raped by the man who was much older than her and the result was her unplanned pregnancy." She said with her heart brimming with emotion.

"And then?" I was grasped in her tale about her mother.

"When she told the news about her pregnancy my father did not accept it as truth. He said it could be from any men with whom she had slept before. However, my mother was sure that it was from him. She was not seeing any customer because of her menstruation. It was that time when my father had raped her."

"That was the worst thing that could happen to anybody. She might have been traumatised". I kept thinking in the back of my mind.

"Did your father really could not believe or he chose not to believe?" I asked.

"He knew about the truth. But in order to save his marriage and maintain the reputation he denied it before all. Later he had threatened my mother saying that if she will open her mouth again he would kill her and the baby too. He took her to his wives and under them she was given proper care until I was born. And in this course of time my mother grew very close to 'Phuchi didi.' She was an elderly woman always looking after my mother. The wives were just there to keep an eye on her and torture her at times in envy for the beauty my mother was."

"But why would they want you? They could have killed you and then your mother could work again." I said.

"The wives were evil. They were so much drunk in jealousy that they killed my mother. They chose to let me live because they would later make me work in the brothel. Just like what I am doing at the present moment."

"How did your father react at her death?" I asked.

"I don't know much about him. Did he love my mother or did he not? When I heard that he killed himself after some days of my mother's death, I was moved within and a question arose what if he loved her? The answer was a mystery then and is a mystery now." She replied.

"What happened to you after that?"

"I grew under the care of Phuchi didi who had also looked after my mother. She was a very loving woman. As I grew up slowly she had started to turn older. She would let me touch her wrinkled skin and heartily she would laugh at my comment.

"I will someday iron your skin and free you from wrinkles." I would say.

"And in return she would hug me close to her bosom and sing to me the songs of the fairies. But the wives were watching over us and how could they see me so happy. Soon I was to turn ten years old. But my tenth year changed my life entirely."

"What was the change?" I questioned.

"At first Phuchi didi described about my mother for the first time and what had happened to her." I broke down into tears.

"But what had pinched my heart more was when she told me that she was leaving. I did not want to believe it. I could never think of going away from her or her going away from me."

"Don't cry beti. She said controlling her own emotions and wiping my eyes with the edge of her Saree. I hugged her and we both cried. The wives banged the door and told her to leave at once. I cried and cried but she left me and I was shut inside the dark room for hours only tears to accompany me."

I could relate myself with Sapna and in many ways we were similar. Both of us had spent our childhood without mother. Sapna was close to Phuchi didi just like I was close to Gayatri once. How strange it was that we both were in the same brothel working as a sex worker.

"What happened to you after that?" I asked again.

"I was forced in a brothel in an early age. Those days are more ghastly than now. Terrified I would try to stay away from men but who could stop a man who is aroused already." She said.

After hearing from Sapna I was sure of one thing that I would never allow my child to work for these people irrespective of its gender. Saheli's condition was becoming clear to me. But how far would it be true?

The next day Saheli called me in to the same place where I was threatened yesterday. This time the wives were not there just the brothel keeper. As I looked at him I thought of Sapna. Just like his father he had two wives too. Was it a coincidence or was he trying to walk on his father's footsteps by doing the exact same thing? However, I was least bothered to know.

"I will let you give birth to the baby but when it turns a year old, your baby will be mine." She said.

I took a while to make a decision.

"I agree." I said with a firm voice.

Both of them were completely surprised hearing my verdict. They would have been so happy. I did not ask the reason which I was already aware of.

"I will not let your plan to be successful" I thought and smirked at them.

"You are my concern now." Saheli said with a statement that I was to stay with her till I would give birth to my baby.

The brothel keeper did not speak a word but just listened.

Twenty One

During the entire period of my pregnancy I was given proper care. I started to stay in a new room larger than before. Time to time Saheli would come to supervise me but with a stern look on her face. Her helper would bring me food and medicines. My life was much better than before. And what had relieved me the most was I no longer had to see men.

Months passed and my stomach grew bigger day by day. Sometimes at night I would howl in pain and when the nightmares would disturb my sleep I would just wake up and stare long towards the sky. I would try to count the stars and in this course I would fall asleep without my own notice. I could feel the slight kick of the baby inside me giving me immense joy.

I did not know whether the rest of the brothel knew about my pregnancy or not. It had been months that I was secluded from them. Even though I had nothing to do but I would not stay idle but talk to my unborn baby. My favourite pastime was to retell the stories which my Grandmother had told me once. And the one which I would usually tell was 'The boy with the magic lamp and 'Soonkeshari Rani or the queen with the golden hair'.

One day as usual in the middle of the night when I was once again awoke by the horrendous dream I chose not to panic. I lay still and later with much struggle holding my baby bump I stretched to look outside the window, it was dark, no stars on the sky and no moon either. Owls had been hooting somewhere. I was scared to close my eyes thinking what if the man who had been chasing me in my dream returns to me again. To get away with my fear I decided to talk with my baby.

At first I rubbed my belly; it was indeed a huge bump. I started then.

"This is to my sleeping child whose breath I wish to count, seeing you my fear and anxiety would go away. Your presence in me gives me new strength and joy. I hope for a clear day where there are no turbulent storms that could crush us. A green meadow where we will walk, with you holding my index finger. Your giggles will sooth my ear which had been listening to the horrors for so long. You know what would I do if I had the magic lamp? I would take you out fast from the den where you are and cradling you in my arms we would disappear to the land of angels." I said.

The baby kicked me this time. I took it as its response. For how much it also would want to see me in the same way as I was longing for it.

The brothel keeper never came to see me neither did his wives. Sapna had continued to rule over my thoughts. The way her mother was murdered, would they murder me too? I was in a difficult juncture witnessing my own life to be so vague. And what about the brothel keeper? Did he know that Sapna was his half sister?

The doctor would come to check me every month. But this time he was not the same old man whose eyes would kindle with love for his patient. It was rather some other person much younger than him.

"Next month." He said.

I looked at him to complete his sentence. But he did not rather start to write something on the paper.

"What is it?" I asked ignoring the fact that Saheli was also standing nearby.

"You will deliver the baby." He said.

I was lying on the bed. My mouth was dry. I became nervous.

When they left I recalled Saheli's keen eyes on my bump. She was more excited than me. On the other hand I was immersed in fear that what would happen now to me and to my baby. My mind was agitated. The promise which I had made to her suddenly started to torment me. In anguish I made a decision. If I could make it real I knew there would be havoc in the lives of all and the brothel would weep in sorrow.

I thought many times before making an attempt. I had been so stirred up with my own opinions that I chose to kill myself and the baby too. But I had to wait for some more days to pass and the next month to arrive.

During this time I had enough conversation with my baby. Tried to make it understand that why I was doing this. And that love sometimes is fatal. Had I not had loved my child so dearly I would have never thought about such an act. But I did because this way I would not push my child into hell knowingly just like my father had done to me. Never did I want to replicate his mistakes again.

So I was waiting patiently to be killed by my own hands. Not only that I was killing my inmost desire to see my baby. So the next month entered. But I was not being able to summon my courage to attempt what I had been aiming for. This way I spent the entire week still trying to beckon myself to act before the time is late.

One fine morning I woke up when still the sun rays were yet to reach the horizon. The time was dusk. I could hear birds chirping outside and cuckoo cooing in a distant land. It reminded me of my friend Arpana with whom I would explore the nature hearing her melodious humming of some rhythm. My bump had become large enough that I had to take support of my one hand to hold it while walking or sitting.

I came to a decision that I would fulfil what I had been thinking for a long time. I planned to starve myself to death. Slowly I went out and reached for the room which was actually a kind of small store room. I latched the door and sat there for hours. I was suffocating as there was only a window which had been closed; I let it be and refused to open it wide. I was cold lying on the floor and panting profusely in pain asking God to have mercy on me. The room was dark with a window. I wanted more air on my lungs. I was choking yet I could not get up and open the window wide. The baby could come out any moment. I bit my hand hard to take control of the agonising situation. I cried out at last unable to hold back what was making me suffer so much.

I only heard the loud thud and someone broke inside the room. Before I lost my senses and eyes closed and everything was dark. Waking up I came across the fact that I had already given birth to my baby. I remembered the promise I had made to Saheli. It alarmed me with fear and so I asked about it. When Rinku brought her to me, for one moment I hated myself for choosing to kill such an infant with dripping innocence.

Rinku told me to rest but I could not. How could I when fears had fettered me and I was disturbed by a chain of questions. How did they break inside the room? Where is Saheli? Why she isn't here when the day finally arrived for which she had been waiting for so long?

After a while the room was empty and Rinku sat by my side cradling my baby in her arms. She then made her sleep inside the cradle and swung it for some time.

"Who brought the cradle?" I asked.

"Saheli had brought it already." She replied.

"Where is she?" I said.

"I don't know."

"Did she see the baby?"

"Yes, she did." Rinku replied.

Both of us were flooded with questions which we wanted to ask to one another. I gave her the first chance to speak. I did not have to give actually. She started in a jiffy.

"Why did you lock yourself?" She asked.

I did not know what to reply to her. Neither did I want to tell her the truth. So I just closed my eyes to what she had been asking me.

"I am sorry." I said with a compassionate face.

Perhaps looking at me she also did not bother to ask me again.

"Don't you do it again?" She said.

"I will never do." I replied with a face of approval.

When I asked Rinku that how they found me here she said that the helper had seen me entering the room who hours later told to Saheli.

"When did you get pregnant?" She questioned me again.

I told her everything and the deal between me and Saheli. The conversation that I had with Sapna regarding her mother frightened her equally. She hugged me tight to comfort me. She also said that she always wanted to see me. She was amazed at my sudden disappearance. And now as the truth was exposed in front of her she was in content.

The baby started to cry. I was in complete ease. Rinku lifted the baby. I knew what she wanted. So I breast fed her and hence I became a mother from a daughter

Twenty Two

After resting for a week I felt I had gained enough strength to start with my post pregnant life in a brothel about which I was indignant. Why would not I be? When all I wanted to do was sit by my baby's side and shower her with kisses. I wanted to answer to her cries by holding her in my arms and caressing her soft skin. But my desire lasted only for some time. I had to return back to my cell.

Since my baby was taken away from me mercilessly and how Saheli did not feel a dearth of pain when I wept grasping her feet. She turned her back towards the promise that we had made. No she did not allow me to keep my baby for a year rather snatched her away from me within a month.

"Don't do this to me." I said to her with my eyes all red with tears.

My heart was torn into two. I was panic-stricken to let go something which was so precious to me. I could not even think of parting away from her. Sometimes life makes us face the ugliest situation which we keep denying and we wish that we never have to stand in front of it.

"You have to start your work soon. I will take care of your daughter." She said.

"But what about your promise?" I said.

"Promises are meant to be broken. Haven't you heard of it before?" She said with a cunning smile on her face.

At first I refused to move and give my baby to her. I looked at her. I felt more in pain. But I would soon rescue her from them no matter how much it would cost me and what troubles would I have to bear.

"Before I go I have a wish." I said.

"And what is that?" Saheli replied.

"I want to name her." I told.

Saheli gave me a surprising look. She nodded her head. I took it as a sign of support.

"Her name will be 'Bhagya' meaning "destiny". I confirmed.

I left silently after that without turning once to look towards my daughter. I held back my tears because I knew what I was up to.

"Meera, wait a second." I heard the treacherous woman calling me from behind.

As I turned back she said "I will let you see Bhagya once a week".

I did not speak a word and just crossed the threshold.

My baby came in my dreams and ruled over my thoughts. Rinku knew what had happened with me and even Sapna who finally came to know the reason why I had been asking about her mother. Once I was back to my previous place I began to work in full swing not only as a hired sex worker but within the brothel too. The more men we would invite to us the more it would make the brothel keeper happy.

"How long has Saheli been here?" I asked to Sapna one day.

"It has been quite some time." She replied.

"Is she related with the brothel keeper in any way?" I questioned.

"They are business partners. She comes from the same village as my father had come." She said.

I did not ask her any further question like why she was not married till now and what happened to her hand? Those were not my concern. But what distressed me every time was about my daughter Bhagya. How she been treating her? I had to free my baby from her as soon as possible.

When the week passed and finally the moment came when I could see my baby. Thankfully she was in a good condition. And when I held her she smiled at me as I tickled her chin with my fingers. At one point I felt like running away from the brothel with my baby. But If I would do that it would make my baby suffer more than me. So I decided to wait for the right time.

I slept with her by my side that night listening to her heart beat and the way she would breathe. Sometimes I would just poke my finger inside her fist. I would feel her warmth and softly I would kiss her forehead.

But the time passed by too fast. When the next day came it saddened my heart again. However I carried hope to see her again and let her go for a while chanting words like 'God, take care of my daughter' in my heart.

To keep the misery at bay I started to spend some part of my day either with Sapna or Rinku. We had developed a very cordial relation in due course of time. When the storm tosses our lives we feel helpless and lose all hope never paying attention to the sacred truth that 'there is a light at the end of the tunnel'. Perhaps I too had thought in that way after going through so much upheaval. Yet I had received now the feeling of companionship in both of them which I had been looking for so long in otherwise empty life of mine.

Deep inside I would yearn for my daughter but again the gleam of hope would smile at me. With them I would laugh rolling in the floor, cry like a baby dream like I was the queen of the world. We would meet secretly. And fortunately the meetings would always be successful and we were not yet caught.

While we were talking amongst ourselves one day I realised that I had to talk something serious. So without taking much time I said

"Let us run away from here."

Both of them looked at me in an abrupt silence.

"Are you serious?" Sapna said with her equally surprised voice.

I nodded my head without speaking anything.

"Where do you want to go?" Rinku asked me.

"I don't know but I just want to run away from here." I said.

"There has to be a proper plan Meera, we just cannot run away wherever we want." Sapna spoke sense which even made me think for a while.

Rinku supported to what she had said with her confirming tone

'Exactly'.

"I have a plan and I am sure that it is going to work. But I need your help." I looked towards both Sapna and Rinku.

"Only after knowing the plan". They both surprisingly answered in chorus.

I told them what I had in my mind with elaborate detail. Just like me even they wanted to be free from the bondage and perhaps the rest of the girls like us. However, at that particular time we just could help ourselves because if anybody would know about it then the outcome would be more dangerous than we could ever think about.

A new dawn arose in our lives suddenly that was giving us enough courage to plot against the brothel keeper and Saheli. Why would not we be happy when it felt as if fate would turn now and the way it would hurl us towards the dark before it seemed as if there was soon going to be a miracle in our lives?

Twenty Three

A nd it was midnight when Saheli had put my baby in the cradle while she was on the bed sleeping. Now her stump was fully visible. It looked very abnormal. I had never seen her that way before. Rinku and Sapna were waiting outside covering themselves with their shawls. I too was covered. So I carefully sneaked inside watching my footsteps that it doesn't make sound.

Bhagya had been sleeping at ease. I lifted her up cautiously so that she don't wake up in the middle of her sleep and start crying. She moved a bit making my heart beat faster. While coming out I heaved a sigh of relief as if I had completed the most difficult task of my life. Previous night we all had conspired well about our plan that we were to follow. We had also included Saheli's attendant who was just a sprouting teenager. She agreed at once when we told her that we were to flee from the brothel as soon as possible.

She had acted clever enough to let the door open so that I could steal my baby away. Not only this, she even packed a bag with all my baby's requirements.

Luck was definitely on our side and perhaps this is why we were not engaged in the work with customers. How strange it was that all three of us were on a day off. Bhagya was still sleeping but she could wake up at any time so before that would happen we had to cross the long corridor adjacent to Saheli's room.

"Are you girls ready?" Rinku asked.

"For what?" Sapna questioned her again.

"To taste the freedom." Rinku told.

"Don't make noise. You will wake up my baby." I wishpered.

None of them spoke after that as if I had casted a spell at them by my words.

Lila who was Saheli's attendant knew every corner of the brothel as she would be seen always wandering around with her. Therefore she led us towards the secret exit that none of us knew before. It was just like the armoire from where I had escaped once. However the stairs were narrow and small. One person could walk at a time. It was down in the basement. We had taken a different way to reach there so we could successfully hide ourselves from the eye of others.

"Didi you go first." Lila told me.

I handed over the bag to her which I had been carrying that contained some clothes. I held Bhagya tight and climbed down with an alert mind and heart. It was pitch dark however I had to wait for all of them to reach me.

And in some time in the mild focus of the torch light that Rinku was carrying we followed Lila. She pushed the door with all her effort. It opened and the sky was gleaming with million stars making the night clear while the moon winked at us that shone in its glory.

None of us could hold back the tears and when we looked to one another all were joyous with teary eyes. We began to walk the unknown way. Bhagya cried aloud at one time. She had actually pooped on her diaper. After we changed her she went back to sleep again nursing on my breasts. Did we look back once? No I don't remember. We kept walking till we were content that we had covered much farther distance from the brothel. All of us had saved some amount of money. If by chance we would end up in any kind of trouble than money would help to seal the people's advances and their lips as well.

It was already decided from before that at first we were to inform the police so he could help us reach some safer place. We decided to hunt for the police station but before that we were all in need of some rest.

"I think that open ground will be safe enough." Sapna said.

And then we lay down in the thin bed sheet chewing some biscuits which we had stolen from Saheli's tin box. It felt divine to rest under the open sky with stars dancing above the head. It reminded me about Sardar's birthday party when thousand lamps had illuminated the sky. We all were awake in complete bliss. The aroma of stillness lingered in the environment. And my Bhagya slept on my chest. I had covered her with a thin cloth so that no insects would bite her and also to save her from the gentle wind.

Back in the brothel we did not know what upheaval would occur. People might come out looking for us. So before that we had to lodge a complaint to the police without revealing our true identity. As there is always a doubt running whether a sex worker is worthy to be offered with a help or not.

The breaking dawn thus reckoned us that it is time now to walk ahead in search of the police station. We had not slept the entire night so the feeling of languor was obvious to show its mark in all of us except my daughter. Our eyes had been puffy and even red. But our rescue was more important at that moment. After walking for sometime Leela sat down on the road.

"Hey, what happened?" I asked.

"I am thirsty." She replied with weary eyes.

We looked around. There were houses. All of us were so lost in our own worlds carrying only one mission to trace the police or the police station that we had forgotten that we had actually reached a market place.

There were not much people around and no hawkers even. In a distance a man was keeping his coconut in stacks for the early buyers. We went to him and bought five of it. At first the man grew nervous to see us all. We looked like travellers. While we were piping the coconut water I looked towards Leela.

"Are you still thirsty?" I asked.

"No." She replied to me.

"Where can we find the police station?" Rinku asked to the man.

He gave us the direction. But at first it was difficult to understand when he included so many turnings. So we asked him for a particular landmark that could make it easier for us.

"It is just opposite to the yellow coloured abandoned building." The man said.

"Where have you come from?" He asked us.

"We missed the bus and now we have lost the way as well." Sapna replied promptly.

"If you wait for some time you could catch a bus from here." He answered.

"No we have lost some of our belongings too." Rinku added confidently.

The man did not ask any more and so we left depending on the direction that he had shown to us.

On the way we had to form a valid excuse that could look real to the policemen.

"So who is going to be what?" I asked.

"We all are cousins. No elaborate relation." Rinku said.

As we neared the yellow building I felt a sudden chill down in my spine. I was afraid to face the policemen and moreover we all were hiding the truth about our identities.

On entering the police station we were greeted by the cold look of the constable with his bulging eyeballs. Just like the one shown in the movies there were several men but I went to the one sitting right in the middle who was busy with his paper works. I was on the lead and the others were behind.

"Excuse me sir." I said rubbing the sweat from my palm. I had given my baby girl to Sapna for a while.

He gave me the impression that he heard my voice and looked at me.

"Yes." His said with his voice so heavy.

"Sir, Can you help us." I asked.

We all stood in front of his desk. While I spoke and the others were taking note of what I would say.

"Please take a seat." He said. I felt that I could trust him.

"Sir, we have somehow managed to escape from a brothel. We don't have a place to go. Could you take us to some place of safety? I have a baby too." I said thus refusing to lie and also betraying my friends to what we had agreed on.

I felt someone nudge me from behind. They were definitely in a state of awe and exasperation. The police inquired me more and nobody lied to him. We all had something to say so that he would be convinced.

"I will see what I can do." He replied.

Thus we were told to wait for some time. In this course all were furious at me.

"Meera, if anything happens to anyone of us then you will be blamed and never forgiven." Rinku said in rage.

Sapna was equally annoyed and so was Lila. I could not find a perfect way to convince them that all would be fine. I too started to doubt the policeman that what if he pushes us to another trap. We all sat on the wooden bench with no hunger and thirst. Everybody was sceptical regarding to what had happened just now. But I did not let myself shrink deep even though I was carrying the fear in me.

The policeman called me again. He had disappeared for a while and as soon as he came back he signalled me with his hand to go towards his desk. I was nervous and worried at the same time. I had just finished nursing my baby who was now with Lila.

"Let us go inside." The policeman said.

I was in a great predicament about the man and to put my trust in him. So I put my blind faith in him and agreed timorously. I don't know whether the girls noticed me walking in with the policeman or not and even I did not care to turn behind.

There was a lady clad in a decent saree. Her red 'bindi' was her trademark that had perfectly matched with her personality. As soon as our eyes met she smiled at me. I too smiled back.

"She is Arunima." The policeman introduced me to her.

"So your name is Meera?" She asked me.

I replied a "yes".

"So how long have you been in the brothel?"

"I was eighteen when I left my home and now I am twenty three." I answered.

I wanted to ask her that who was she. But I refused to interrogate. She had a certain charm in her personality. And even the police man showed her respect. I was keen to know who that suave lady was.

"Are they your friends who are sitting outside?"

"Yes. We all are from the same brothel. I have a baby daughter too."

She was not astounded to hear about my baby. And that is what I had not expected.

"I have a safe refuge for you all. Do you want to come with me?"

I was to become happy, effulge with joy. But I was not. May be it was because I had been tumbling down in to the cruel hollow all this while. Thus I went back to the same confusing state of mine to decide what could be right for me.

"Life cannot be harsh to you always." My grandmother had said once.

So keeping my faith on her words I approved to her approach.

And then she came towards me and hugged me tight. I was in peace. The policeman left us alone in the room.

And her words added colours and air in otherwise sunken life of mine. At that moment I wanted to shout aloud to Parul who had once asked me about the existence of angels.

I would say "Yes dear, I met with an angel who waved a magic wand in my life and from an ugly ogre transformed me into a beautiful soul."

Twenty Four

From a tiny insect to the trees around it felt as if they had a story to tell. The tale would be about love, friendship and joy. The way tall trees swung made me feel as if they were waiting to invite us from so long. And now we were really safe under their shade. We no more had to burn in the fire of the hell that we each had experienced in the brothel. The flowers that bloomed around wiped off the tears from our eyes. The very moment I entered our safe haven it reminded me about my own dream that I had dreamt about when for the first time I was in Sahib's bungalow with my father and sisters. Its beauty was captivating too.

Arunima introduced us to her 'Cheli beti". She was a nepali woman and thus her organisation was in her native dialect which meant 'sisters and daughters'. The ambience was welcoming so were her rescue team who greeted us with warm embraces. One of them carried my daughter with compassion.

"She looks just like you." She told me.

I replied her back with a wide smile on my face.

The journey so far of my life was tumultuous but even when the storm tossed and turned me I never did sink. There were other girls and women like us with their own sob story. Never had I realised before that I was not the only victim of dreadful fate. Rinku, Sapna and Lila were equally rejoicing as they wept to see their life in the verge of sweeping change. And this time life had good things for us in store and no more mistreatment by anybody.

It had taken a night to reach Arunima's place. We had travelled by bus. She took good care of all of us and fed us till we had to say that we were full. She denied any further questions regarding the brothel after she had asked us individually.

"Life will be different now." She exclaimed in the end.

And inside "Chelibeti" we had to maintain the routine. My baby daughter started to grow in a healthy environment. We made new friends but Rinku, Sapna and Lila were still close as before to me.

With Arunima we felt as if we were reborn to a new mother. She would dance with us and teach us to sing. Her efforts were blooming to engage us in various activities so that the past nightmares will not lead us towards depression. There were girls affected with many diseases. And one of them was Sapna too detected with HIV. But never were any of them treated differently. Though the precautions were maintained but at the back of our minds we were well conveyed with the message that all were equal before the eyes of God and that nobody chooses to be sick or suffer with any kind of sickness. So why detach the people?

When Sapna was diagnosed with the virus, she came running to me in tears. I knew something had gone wrong with her. So I just listened to her.

"Meera, I am dying a slow death." She said.

"What are you saying?" I asked.

"The doctors confirmed today that I am suffering with HIV."

I looked at her in fright. However I had to hide my emotion so I tried to stay calm.

She broke down in tears making me equally moved. Eventually I cried holding her too. Later she even refused to eat. As always Arunima waved her magic wand at her by her soothing words and miraculously she became jovial again.

That night she visited our dormitory. She sat in the middle and we circled her.

"You all are lost stars." She said.

And nobody could understand the depth of her statement. So we all kept quiet.

"Stars are not only that shine in the sky. We all are stars in our own way. Some succeed to shine while some not, some are found while some are always lost."

"Then why are we still referred to as lost stars?" Naina asked who had been rescued from another brothel few days before us.

"It is because though you all are found now; you continue to remain lost by brooding over your past. Develop your skills and shine. Try to radiate light in all the darkness that you all have been through." She uplifted us with her ushering words.

So from the next day a new energy surged in all to hone the skills and develop it. Some were good in embroideries while some in knitting. In this way we all were involved in one or the other activity.

I loved gardening. Whenever I would be engaged in it I remembered Baba. Perhaps it was one of the reasons why I was so much drawn towards it. And when in the season the flowers bloomed I praised my own hands though secretly.

One day I took out the note now wrinkled which was given to me by the lawyer. Nobody could read it fluently till now so I decided to show it to Arunima who was then playing with my daughter in the garden outside.

"What is it?" She asked me.

I fondled Bhagya's cheeks when I carried her in my arms.

"I was given this note by the lawyer whom I had met long time ago. He was one of my customers." I said.

"So you want me to read it?" She questioned me again.

"Yes. Will you?" I urged to her.

She sat down in the wooden stool and managed her spectacles. I too sat beside her with Bhagya on my lap.

"Thank you for the peaceful night." She read.

All this while I had thought that a secret message would be written on the note. But it was just a mere thank you which had led us to take great difficulty while reading it.

"What had you done so special Meera that he left a thank you note for you? Arunima asked.

I described her entire incident about that day hearing to which even she made a face of pity for the poor fellow.

"Poor thing." She remarked.

Later in the evening I met with Sapna, Rinku and Lila. We all sat together sharing the wonderful experiences that we were living every moment in spacious 'Chelibeti'.

"Thank you Meera." Rinku said.

"For what?" I replied.

"For bringing us here." Lila added.

"I did not bring you here it was all destiny. We managed to reach the end of the dark tunnel." I said with a smile on my face.

"Truly life is like a mystery box." Sapna said.

Twenty Five

That afternoon it had rained heavily. I was sitting by the window sill alone so lost in my own thoughts. The view outside was serene and fresh. I took it as a sign of rejuvenation. The drops made a spattering sound on the roof scaring the birds away. I opened the window and put out my hand outside to feel the rain. The drops wet my hands immediately. I sprinkled on my face too. I saw two magpies taking shed under the bush. And a dog that would be strolling around otherwise was cleaning himself with the help of his tongue. Sometimes he would also shake the water off from his body.

I had started to be homesick. I had actually gone back to that time when I danced in the rain along with my sisters. As soon as the rain would start to drizzle Parvati would call us on top of her voice.

In disgust I would say "Only a strand of your hair will be wet. Call me that time when I could be totally drenched."

When the roaring thunder would intervene I felt so vivacious and then I would go out and wait for the first heavy drop to hit me. My wait would be always worthwhile. On the heavy rain I would escape from all my worries. Seeing me even my sisters would come barefaced pointing towards the sky.

I felt an uncontrollable urge to meet all of them. To see how much my sisters have grown up by now. My Baba whom I had left cursing made me think that whether he suffered after leaving me or not. I did not want to think much about my step-mother. She might have been blissfully happy after I left from home. And my dear friend Arpana with whom I made some everlasting memories. I also wanted to find out about Gayatri who just disappeared mysteriously.

I felt that now the time was right to unravel everything. So I made up my mind that I will visit my village and see what the new changes there are. I also wanted to live again in those old bygone days of my life.

Arunima was helping a young girl tie her hair. I interrupted in the middle. She signalled me with her hand to wait for a while.

"Tell me." She said as if she knew what I had to say from before.

My hands were sweaty. I felt awkward to tell her because I did not know whether she would permit me or not. But I had to summon my courage anyhow. Clearing my throat I looked at her eyes.

"Arunima, I want to go home for a while." I said.

She was perplexed to hear what I just said to her. I was more tongue-tied in her silence which only lasted for a minute long. She knew which place I belonged to.

"Do you know how far your home from here is?" she questioned me.

"No, I don't." I answered.

"It is just few hours away. You can go anytime." She said with a beaming face.

That moment what amazed me more was not just her approval but the fact that I was staying so close to my home yet I always felt that I was in some distant corner of the country.

"Thank you Arunima." I said and hugged her tightly.

I could not sleep the whole night after that. I was having mixed feelings. I was unsure that how my family would treat me once they will see me with my daughter. And they would go through a great turmoil once they would hear about how Bhagya was born and that she was fatherless.

Nevertheless I was ready to answer to every difficult question. I had to take it as a great challenge and to not feel guilty about my past. I had not chosen it rather I was forced. I always reminded this truth about myself. As I was preparing to leave with Bhagya that morning I could not understand my edgy feeling within. Was it because I was going back to my village after so long?

Arunima had told me to take care of myself and my daughter before I left from there. She gave me some amount of money that I took with a willing heart. As I turned back to get a glimpse of her Arunima had already gone inside. So

I shifted my gaze to the window and saw Rinku, Sapna and Lila waving me goodbye.

"I am not going for ever." I felt like shouting at them.

Yet I remained quiet and just smiled back. I would come back to them. That is what I had decided too.

Hari was accompanying me till the bus stop. He was with me on Arunima's advice. We reached the place and he also showed me the seat where I was to sit for next couple of hours. He then wished me a safe journey and left after receiving a polite thank you from my side. I held Bhagya close to me. My mind had been flooding with numerous thoughts. I was soon to meet my family. I tried to calm myself down and not think about any such things at least for a while.

So I leaned against my seat and closed my eyes. There were passengers slowly filling up the empty seats. The vehicle was to move any time. Just a few miles of distance and soon the gap of long departure from my loved ones would be filled. As anticipated the bus left with a soft roar as the driver twisted the keys. I took a deep breath to help me deal with my ongoing nervousness.

The cool wind messed up my hair and thus the strands were sweeping through my bare neck. I had been looking outside the window. Every single object outside was passing by so fast. At some point that time I felt the place was familiar. It just reckoned to me that I had already entered my village. The bus stopped in the chaos. I knew the way but it was to my utmost surprise that it had changed so fast. The once muddy streets looked smooth making it a well made road. The houses and shops had mushroomed too. I felt a deeper connection with the place now yet I was also feeling alienated from the entire surrounding. I was the last one to get down from the vehicle. I decided to walk myself to home. So I began to walk having a conversation with myself.

Already the village I knew was dividing into two. I started to compare to what it was before and what it had become now. The tea gardens were green as ever. I stopped on the edge of an elevated land. I looked around to see from where the voluminous smoke was coming from. And then I spotted a scale of huge constructions which made me curious to know that what it was actually. There was nobody around me so I just kept the question in my mind and coin it when I meet anybody later. It was definitely not the time of monsoon so the rivers could just rise up to the level of an ankle. I wished to see Sahib's bungalow too. For that I had to wait until I reach my home.

My Baba always loved me. It was just he could not show his emotions. That day when he had left me with Rajan I could well understand from his face that how hard was it for him to knowingly submit me to another man. Yet I hated him that time for his deeds. Perhaps I was too young to understand that truth is always not what we think. But truth is what we see. If I could look at his eyes that time I would definitely feel his pain. I had already forgiven him. I could not make my words come true which I had thought about when I was leaving with Rajan.

But now the time had come to reconcile everything and to let go whatever had taken place earlier. I was looking for a new beginning but would everybody nourish themselves with the same feeling? I had understood that holding grudges always make one burdened. Forgiveness is the key to the inner peace. And this I realised from a simple story shared to us by one of the girls back in 'CheliBeti'. She had forgiven her husband who had sold her to a brothel when she could not bear him any child. And then I asked her that very moment

"So now you have forgiven him, do you plan to stay with him again?"

She looked at me for a while and replied.

"Forgiveness does not mean that you have to be the same person again. It is just you are releasing yourself from the bondage of carrying anger towards someone in you. When you forgive you let go and become cautious of not repeating the same mistake again. If I become the same person again I will repeat my mistake. I will give the other person the same chance to do the same thing which he had done to me before."

I was so touched by what she had said to me. From that moment onwards I decided to forgive every single person who had done badly to me. And thus as I was walking towards my home I was ready to embrace all with an open heart.

Bhagya had also come out of her sleep by now. I wished to read her mind to find out what she might be thinking or thinking not at all. She would meet her own very soon and play in my sister's lap. I entered the narrow lane. I was just few steps away. It did not amaze me at all to hear my heart beating so fast.

Twenty Six

A girl had been scrubbing the charcoal coated kettle outside with all her might and rapt attention. I could not see her face but just her back. Her hair was long which she had braided and it extended till her waist. Was she one of my sisters? I was yet to find it out. But before I would approach her she wheeled back. I noticed her blank expression and a cold look of a stranger. My head whirled. She was certainly not my sister but what was she doing at my home. A man in his middle age came out munching something in his mouth. I did not know him either. Who were these people? What were they doing at my home? I was inquisitive to know everything.

They kept staring until I broke the silence.

"I am here for my family." I said.

The girl looked at the man herself not being able to answer what I had said to her.

"This is our home." The man replied.

I was amazed at his reply. I clearly remembered where I belonged. I knew the roof and the muddy walls. The cow shed outside was in the same place. That iron log where my dad would sit and smoke was kept in the same position. Only the log had been started to rust and had greatly changed its colour. How fast the man was taking ownership of everything.

"Where is my father?" I asked to him.

He still wore the look of blank expression. Did he really did not know about it or was he just pretending not to know? He did not reply to what I had asked him.

"Come inside." The man said.

I went in and found everything the same. It was my house but where was my father and my sisters? A lady came from inside with a glass of water but again she was also a total stranger to me like the rest.

I sat with my baby daughter on the stool and drank the water. All three of them sat near to me. I felt uncomfortable.

"This house was abandoned before we shifted here." The man said.

"Was there nobody?" I asked.

"No, we just found some of their belongings." The woman replied.

It felt as if somebody had pushed stabbed me. I did not know in what way I to take it was. But I chose to remain calm in order to find out the sudden disappearance about my family. Now that we were strangers so I had to introduce myself to them. I told them about my past but I kept the truth about my past identity as a secret.

"So when did your husband die?" The lady asked me. She had believed in my made up story.

"He died a week later when my daughter was born." I replied in a very confident way.

"Where are you from?" I questioned to them.

"We are from Jaigaon. After Gayatri's death we could not stay there for long. Her memories would often haunt my daughter. She was very close to her. In fact when my daughter was born she was the one to keep her name."

The name which the lady had pronounced sounded very familiar to me.

"Was she blind?" I asked her.

"Yes, she was. How do you know about it?" She asked me eagerly.

I was sure that they had been talking about my Gayatri whom I had left a long time ago. I stood frozen when I heard about her.

"Don't just brief me. I want to know everything in detail." I said.

The man seeing me so eager told me that Gayatri was bleeding that night. She was terrified and alone leaning by an electric pole. Nobody was there with her and when asked she just said that she was left there by her brother. Had she not been blind may be she could find her way to her home again. But due to lack of vision she was much more helpless. Out of pity the man brought her to his home. His wife was pregnant then. Next morning they found out that Gayatri knew a lot of things and did not appear as vulnerable as the blind person. So she began to stay with them as a help. She helped them in many ways though she was unable to provide much help physically but she was a great support during the times of turmoil. Often the pregnant lady would spend her time with Gayatri hearing her stories and good times spent with her beloved 'Meera'. That person was definitely me. And I would well understand how much she longed to see me as I would after we were separated from one another.

"And how did she die?" I asked again.

"She was detected with tuberculosis. She died in the hospital after a week." The man replied.

When they finally learnt that I was that 'Meera' of Gayatri they were happy to welcome me at their home. They even told me to stay with them unless I don't find about my family. I also found out that their daughter had the same name as mine.

"Now we know the reason why Gayatri chose that name for our daughter." The lady said.

"Are you sure that the house was empty when you first came here?" I asked to the man.

"There was nobody here. I remember a person who brought us. She was a young married woman." He said.

"What is her name?" I asked again.

"Nani." He replied.

I wondered about the name. It sounded strange to me. 'Nani' meant 'the little one' in Nepali. I felt that her name could possibly be something different.

"Do you know where does she stay?" I said.

The man confirmed a "Yes".

That night I dined with them and later the lady allowed me to see through each rooms of my house. I went there silently. And in the quietness I tried to listen to the echo of my sisters' laughter. I had been completely broken to encounter the void. It pained me each time to think that I had suffered the loss of my loved ones. Gayatri's death was heart rending to hear. The faces for whom I had come searching seemed to vanish and their smell did not even linger in the air. And this is why they say that memories not only give joy to a person but it also kills the joy. I wanted to forget the time that I had spent with them but now they were engraved in my mind. I wished to break free from them but I could never do it.

Bhagya had already slept. I no more carried the same feeling of euphoria because the hopes and the anticipation that I was having the very morning were suddenly wiped out. I thought for whom should I live for? And why is happiness so temporary in life?

As always I could not sleep well neither could I be patient. I just wanted the sun to dawn as fast as it could. Will tomorrow would ignite the light of hope or push me toward more pain. I certainly had no answer for it.

And then I saw the same old magnificent bungalow from outside where I would come often with my father. The several times I had passed by it with Arpana and sometimes we had even plucked the flowers only to tug them inside our hair and act like a princess. Once we were caught by the gatekeeper while we had been trying for the ripe litchis.

We thought the man would scare us away rather he got us a bunch of juicy litchis and that was enough for both of us to put on a smile until we had reached home. All the way we ate it and danced and frolicked. I wanted to go inside but I did not.

"Who stays here?" I asked to the man who had come along with me in my search for Nani.

"The new owners of the tea estate." The man replied.

Bhagya cradled in my arms. I had brought her along with me.

"Do you want to rest for some time?" the man asked.

I said 'no' and thus we began to walk. During that time I told him about the days that I had spent here. He listened to me quietly. Later he also shared about his sad tale that how he had lost his first born. And that he belonged to an affluent family but when there was rift between the brothers for the inheritance he found it wise to just let go.

"Why did you leave everything?" I questioned to him.

"More than the riches I yearned for inner peace. The conflicts that I would have every day at home had started to ruin my mental stability. And there is nothing to take away from this world when you die. I choose to smile even in my deathbed. So I just gave away and planned for a new beginning in this small village. Luckily I found a house for free." The man answered.

"How do you earn your living now?" I asked.

"I have opened a small shop in the main market." He said.

How a man who had everything before could find his happiness in a small hut and in few wages that he would earn daily. The transformation was miraculous. But did he really mean what he said to me? I doubted him.

Then out of the silence that had prevailed for a minute long, Bhagya began to cry. I tried to comfort her but she continued to cry. The man took her from me and made her rest on his broad hands forming a cradle where he began to swing her slowly to and fro. And thus the chirpy cry changed to cackling laughter. I smiled too.

"Are you tired?" the man asked.

"A bit tired." I answered.

"We are almost there." He said.

We had covered quite a distance. We still were walking when suddenly I stamped over the pot hole making my feet dirty. It reminded me of something that had happened some years earlier. An old friend came in my thought that had unknowingly made me cringe when the muddy water drew some streaks on my face when her cycle bumped over a pothole.

Twenty Seven

To my surprise it was nobody but Arpana. People would fondly call her 'Nani'. She looked completely different. The man was surprised to see that we already knew each other so well before he could introduce. I hugged her in joy. We just could not speak a word for a while. Then later she took my baby and kissed her gently. I knew there were many things that she would want to ask me. I was equally curious to know about her.

"Do you know her?" The man asked me.

"Yes I do. She is my childhood friend." I replied.

The man thought us leaving us on our own and I assured to him that I will be fine.

"You can come to our place anytime later." He said and thus left.

Arpana lived with her two kids and a husband who seemed to be nowhere at that moment. On asking her I found out that it had been months that he was away from home. The reason was to earn more to fulfil the burning desires of his family. If there was a man like Pukar who was satisfied with his simple life than there was also someone like Arpana's husband who felt the little money was not enough to suffice the needs of the family. The difference was remarkable. And this is why a whole lot of men often chose to hunt for minor jobs outside leaving their families behind. I could notice the fear hidden beneath Arpana's eyes which she tried to hide by looking elated. Fear that what if her man don't return to her.

Later that evening we sat together outside in the open veranda of her home. I had Bhagya sleeping next to me in a small cot while her sons were off to play. The tea provided us with the warmth in otherwise chill atmosphere.

"That day I had come to search for you. I was deeply wounded to know that I would soon be married to someone who was double my age. The only person I could think at that time was you. I remember the look on your Baba's face when I asked him about you. He said you would never return again and you were gone forever. I was terrified to hear about it. Nobody replied to me even when I nagged them. All were muted and your sisters they were clueless like me. I spent the night howling in pain, cursing God for such misfortune." Arpana said.

I did not say a word but just looked at her. So that she could speak what she had been longing to tell me for such a long period of time.

"I was married to him in spite of my agitation. Only because the man was rich. He was a retired army and easily got drawn to me when he visited our liquor shop. My mother soon gave up selling tea and snacks instead she encouraged the new business and found it more profitable."

"And you supported her?" I asked angrily.

"I had no other option. She was my mother after all. Many men began to gamble in our shop and all the time it would be a chaos. I felt so disturbed. If you remember it had been weeks that we had not met after our last time together near the river. I was actually sinking inside a sea of trouble. When that man entered our shop I had substituted my mother that day. He fell for me and in no time he proposed me for marriage. I turned down the offer but my mother was lured. I felt I was actually sold to him for a hefty sum of money."

"Where was he from?" I questioned to her.

"He had his relatives in the village. He had come to see them from some state of the country. He would speak an unusual language. In no time I was married to him and thus he began to stay with us. The man just indulged in drinking and sex. I could never know that he had a family somewhere or not. We never talked much. At first I could not accept the fact that I was partnered with such an old man. A year passed. I had just given birth to my first son and the tragedy took place. However whatever happened I call it a good luck."

"What happened then?" I was eager to know.

"He died." She said.

"How did he die?"

"He died a sudden death early morning. And it was because of the excessive intake of the alcohol. We found him on the table with the bottles by his side. He had puked blood."

"It was a very tragic death indeed." I said.

"But his death at least ended the abuses. I was no more exploited sexually. I began to work in the construction site which soon was transformed into chain of industries."

"So that is where the smoke comes from?" I questioned.

"Yes. Half the people from the village go there to work these days." She replied.

Everything had changed so fast. And yet so much turmoil had been in Arpana's life too. We indeed have our own share of troubles.

"That is where I met Sandeep, my husband." She said.

I looked at her. She grinned at me.

"The daily encounters that we would have at the site strengthened our bond. He was my only friend there. People began to talk about us but who could stop us? We had become very cordial to each other. He lived alone. His parents had already passed away. Even after knowing about my baby he never tried to judge me like the others."

When she talked about Sandip her eyes lighted in joy. No more could I see the wrath in her.

"One day as usual we were returning back from the site. The time was evening. I would always take my baby boy to work. I was unsure about my mother's care. He was still tiny and in Sandip's hand. I had been in love with him but unable to confess before him. I had the fear of being rejected and especially in my case. He would never accept a girl like me as I was already married before with a son. However my thoughts did not match with the reality."

"Did he propose you then?" I asked to her.

"Yes he did. The words blurted out from his mouth so sudden that made me shiver in excitement."

"So what was your response?"

"My response was that in a week's time I got married to him." She replied.

"That is a lovely story." I appreciated her.

"The other son is from him." She told me.

And then I found out from Arpana that both of them started to work in the same place where they had been working earlier. She left her mother and her home. However she visits her sometimes who still runs the same liquor shop.

"After Sandip has left, I have started to fear about many things?" Arpana said.

"Like what?" I questioned her.

"Fear about the future and most of it the fear of losing him." She said.

"I understand." I replied to her.

But did I really understand? I was never in love with anybody. The very essence of love itself was alien to me. I had in me the love for my loved ones. But I wondered how it feels to be in love with a man whom you give the consent to be the owner of your body. And whom you call the other half of you.

"Tell me about you. Where have you been for so long?" Arpana asked me zealously.

I took a deep breath and paused for a minute. I began to question my mind that from where should I start my story. Will it be good if I don't tell her that I was involved in sex trade? Yet I decided that I would tell her everything. So I had been the mysterious diary for sometime before and now she was exposed to every pages of my life. From the very moment when I was given away by my father to Rajan and the encounters that I had with Gayatri, Sardar and his grandchildren and Mantu. And then how the chronicle of the dark world of prostitution had started in my life. The sudden traps that I fell into leading towards my pregnancy and the final escape to 'Cheli Beti'.

Arpana was dumbstruck to hear about this. I wondered what she would be thinking. Would she hate me now for speaking the truth? I expected her to shun me away but she did not.

"It amazes me to know that you are so courageous." She said.

"What makes you think that?" I asked.

"Had I been in your place I would never have been able to survive after bearing such brutal tortures."

"I had no choice." I said.

"What kept you alive?" She asked again.

"I had a hope that I would be free from the shackle someday." I answered.

And then I asked her the most awaited question.

"Where are my parents and sisters?"

"They had to leave the place." Arpana replied.

"Why is that?" I asked.

"Last year few people came in our village for a survey. They went door to door inquiring about the citizenship in the country. Since your father had come from Nepal so that made him a refugee here. There were other people too who were caught for the same reason. Some had come from the neighbouring country like Bhutan. This created a hue and cry and the surveyors decided to report the case to the police. And thus the police came with an order to take all the so called refugees to the refugee camp in Nepal from where they would be taken by the powerful country like America as labourers."

I sat stunned. Just now I had overcome the trauma. I was not ready to face the other one again. Tears welled up in my eyes and slowly it ran down my cheeks. This time the pain inside was rare. It felt as if my heart could come out any moment. I wanted to pull my hair and roll around on the ground, beat my chest and cry. I felt like ending my life then and there without caring about anything. I wished I could break free from the grim reality that I could never see anyone of them again. Why is pain so torturous? I did not want to suffer knowing the fact that in some distant land is my family yet I could never meet them again. I wanted to die the very moment. But would my soul rest in peace even after the death? It would never be. I had to face the truth. I was to suffer in this fire of loss.

Twenty Eight

I wished it was just a dream, a bad dream. Had it been then I would wake up and find my loved ones. I would hug them tight without making them aware of what I had gone through. My tears would dry then, the agony within would be no more there. Perhaps I could not then get so emotional every time and to close my eyes would not have been so hard. My voice would not choke while talking to someone. I would stop being so lost.

But it was real, a sad truth of my separation with them whom I could never see, never hear again neither touch and feel the warmth of love.

Arpana sat beside me the entire night trying to relieve me by speaking soft words. In an attempt to heal my pain she tried to tell me a story.

"In a distant forest were many oak trees. In one of them lived two birds as they had built their nest there. They were inseparable and flew together all the time. During daytime those two parrots would pick on the ripe guavas and return back to their shelter when it was dusk. But one day while they were flying together a hunter shot one of them. The parrot fell fluttering its wings. The other one helpless at the situation flew where his friend was fallen. The hunter then captured the parrot in the cage and threw the dead one away."

I was silent and just listened to her story.

"So what is the moral of the story?" I asked.

"Just like you were born alone so did the parrot was hatched out of the egg alone. When we are in a company of somebody we forget that this will be for temporary. Separation is fated in the lives of all be it a bird or a human."

For some time I was motivated by what Arpana had just told me but how could I forget that how fragile was my heart.

In the morning as I lay beside Bhagya the same statement was repeating inside my mind.

"You have a daughter now. You have to be strong for her." Arpana had told me.

So I decided to go back to 'Cheli-Beti' for the more I would stay there the more I was prone to get poignant thoughts. I felt like an orphan now and more than that like a handicapped person. Yet I had my biggest strength, my daughter and one day I would share all the tales of my life. How would she react then? Would she shy away or shun me as her mother? But I had to believe and wait for everything to be fine and patiently wait for her to transform.

I had told Arpana that I would leave tomorrow so it was my last day. We planned of visiting the riverside where we had gone when we were teenagers. It would be like a dry picnic. She prepared so snacks and we all headed together with few things. She with her sons by her side and I was cradling Bhagya.

On reaching there I found not many changes except the air was not so clean and pure that it used to be. The smoke continued to blow out of the huge chimneys of the industries. We spread the mat and sat there while the boys played with the ball. Arpana supervised them not to go too far and I understood her motherly concern.

We began to talk about many things. I shared some of my ghastly experiences back in the brothel. I told her that the brothel keepers show no shame to commit such terrible crime. All that matters to them is money. And that many innocent girls fall prey to such monsters that devour them with the help of other men. But however none can defy their soul. And perhaps this was why I could survive and escape from there.

"I have a name for you." Arpana suddenly said.

I grew nervous and felt what it could be. Good or bad?

"What is it?" I asked.

"The Unsung Heroine." She answered.

I smiled and reflected on the name. But I could not coin a perfect meaning out of it.

"What does that mean and how does it get connected to me?" I questioned curiously.

"Listen carefully". She said.

She perfectly explained me the sense behind the name.

"Take an example of a beautiful pair of shoes. When you buy it the design attracts all so easy. All are curious to know about the designer. But what about those hands which polish it, help in gluing the shoals and even cutting the scraps of leather or fabric? They are thus the unsung group. Nobody praised them but they have a value. Similarly, you are an unsung heroine representing all the girls who have fallen prey to the flesh trade. It is because all look down upon the sex-workers but do they know how strong they are to let go their own pain and give pleasure to others. They sacrifice their own self and identity to make others rich. Be it a brothel keeper who earns riches through all of his workers or the common man who grow rich in by acquiring the complete satisfaction by being served in the most pleasurable ways as possible." Arpana told me without a sigh. It felt as if she spoke in one breath.

I was exulted and she boasted my self esteem.

"So what do you think? Does it make you the unsung heroine?" She questioned me again.

I was so elated to reply to her "Yes, It does."

And then at night I slept in peace from the days of languor. The pain would remain within always but each day I had to battle with it in a dauntless courage. The very next day I left with nothing more but just a beaded necklace in different colours which Arpana gifted me as a token of love. She stood on the doorstep. She had tears in her eyes and waved me goodbye till I was a thin shadow in a distant road. I thought of taking the last glance of my home so I went and greeted all three of them. I did not know whether I would return back or not and even if I would after how many years? Will the house remain same? Perhaps I would see a different form in place of the present thatched and muddy hut. And then it will be just a story that there lived a family whose house is now taken away.

"When will you come again?" The lady asked me.

I wished I could avoid that question and tell her that I too had been seeking answer for it.

Yet I replied "I don't know."

After receiving the good luck wishes for my future I departed with a cold heart. I revived all the memories once again of that ill-fated day when I was taken away by Rajan. I wished I had been strong back then and would have agitated. I wished I had not been so naive. I was to blame for the bitter consequences that followed next. For how long would I carry the burden of anger towards my father? I wanted to break free from the bondage.

"I forgive you father". I whispered as if the words would reach his ears. But I believed that it reached. Was my belief not enough?

Bhagya's little hands touched my cheeks as if giving me the assurance that I am not alone in this world. She was there with me though small but one day she would grow tall and be my pillar of strength as she was now.

The bus moved in a jiffy. This time I had to find my own way to 'Cheli Beti'. I knew that I wouldn't be lost. I had well noticed the landmarks when Hari had accompanied me before.

Twenty Nine

As expected Rinku ran towards me and took Bhagya in her arms and showered her with kisses. I left my daughter with her and went to find Arunima. She was monitoring some new girls who looked at me in surprise when I interrupted them in the middle of their meeting.

"Give me some time Meera." Arunima requested.

I nodded and went out and sat on a stool for her to call me again. What I was to tell her that my parents are gone in some distant land? Should I name myself as the lonely orphan because I lost my family even when they are alive? While I played with such thoughts I got a call from inside.

"How are you?" Arunima asked with a hug.

I couldn't hold myself back so I cried aloud. She perhaps would have been amazed to see my sudden outburst. But she did not inquire but patted my back silently. She understood that something was very wrong with me. Later when I stopped crying she made me sit handing me a glass of water.

"Will you tell me now?" She said.

I told her about my loss and how overwhelmingly sad I was. She did not try to comfort me with pleasing words but just gave an ear to what I had to say.

Later she told me that this is what life is all about. Life is indeed an equal balance of pain and sorrow.

"But I think many will not agree with it especially the less fortunate one like me."

"Have you seen your future? You don't know what it holds for you." She replied.

"I think a mountain of sorrows." I said.

"This is where you go wrong and you fail to identify the good things that are in store for you."

"How can you be so sure about it?"

"I just believe. Sometime all you need to do is put your faith and trust upon the unknown even when you don't see. Who knows when your belief turns into a reality?" She said.

"So should I believe that I may meet with my family someday?"

"The choice is yours. Your belief must not carry any expectation. You have to be brave enough to face anything. This way you will never be hurt and depressed."

This was the beauty of Arunima that when she spoke it always touched our hearts. And she was our great inspiration and a constant motivation. She never failed to encourage anybody.

From that day onwards I chose to rise again from all that I had suffered. I actively participated in the activities and my bond with my three friends Rinku, Sapna and Lila was still close. They knew what misfortune I had faced yet they stood by me in all my trials.

SOME YEARS LATER

Thirty

The birds are chirping around. It is a pleasant day and my story has just ended. I wipe tears from the corner of my eyes. The ink blots due to the droplets of tears that fell down from her eyes too on the thin sheet of paper. As I had recalled my past it has made me emotional that even to keep an eye contact with her for a minute I feel that the sea of emotions would flood out any moment. I take a deep breath and calm myself down. All this while I had realised my worth so I did not build any room for self pity. Fearlessly I face her. She is still looking at me.

"What is she thinking? No I am not the poor creature so don't feel sorry for me. I have rose high from all I have been through. I have learnt to respect myself. We are sitting under the clear blue sky. She scribbles something on the paper again. I notice the hand movement. She writes so fast. I have also managed to learn the basics. I can well write the alphabets but it will take time for me to run my hand so fast. But I will learn sooner.

When she first came to me I was detangling my unruly hair taking the warmth of the sun. She had come with a group of friends from a foreign land. Her name is Laura. They have come to visit 'Cheli Beti'. So she greeted me with a warm smile. Her green eyes grabbed my attention. She had neatly tied her blonde hair. To my surprise she knew my language. I was amazed to witness her speak fluent Nepali. The day before their arrival we were told by Arunima about them. She had said only a selected few will share their stories with them. I did not want to be one of them. But life often makes us expect the unexpected.

We started informally. It took me a while to be comfortable with her but before she asked anything. I asked her.

"How are you so fluent in this dialect?"

She did not let the smile fade away.

"I am studying your language. I am living in Nepal for past five years." She replied.

I praised her enthusiasm but did not let it reach her ears. And then she told me that she wanted to know about my past life which was obviously intertwined with pain, suffering and struggle. Why was she so curious to know about my life? I felt like asking her but held myself back just realising the fact that I had to trust Arunima. She had let these people talk to us so there could be a good cause. But I had tried so hard each day to ease my pain, the wound had taken years to dry yet the scar remained. As sometime even the mere scar is enough to make it realise that how fatal was the wound. My scar within was still prominent. It could probably not fade away. Now I was put in such a situation where I had to dig up my old scar and that turn back to the chapters of the closed book of my life. I was not so willing to do it. Yet I decided to open to that chapter of my life as a child back in Nepal and thus I started.

"From the days of my early childhood I was always in search of a better pursuit of my life."

And thus she listened to me with rapt attention. And time to time wiping her tears. I opened up to her so naturally that it did not feel a moment that she was actually a total stranger to me till she introduced herself to me.

She knew my name so I did not find it a necessity to give her my introduction. I was given respect by her which meant a lot to me.

Breaking the awkward silence she looks at me and a smile glows once again on her face. I too smile back this time.

"I am sorry to hear about your friend." She says.

I tell her that her name was Sapna and that she was suffering from HIV. I declare her to be a person with a brave heart. She never complained about anything but only one time did she actually cry when first she met with her ghastly disease from the person who proved to her that she was an HIV victim. We saw how she changed from a tall and chubby girl which she once was to a frail and thin figure.

I also tell Laura that what Sapna wished for after she was dead. She wanted her body to be buried in the premises of 'Cheli Beti'. And flowers to be grown around her grave. No wonder her wish is granted. Laura urges me to take her to the grave. I agree and we both walk and there we see a cemented platform painted in red. In it Sapna's name is written and flowers bloom around. I notice a rose on her grave.

"This is for me from Sapna." I assume and tell Laura.

She agrees with me in my assumption and says "Yes it is."

We go back and sit on the same bench where we had our long conversation. Laura tells me about her own life and that she was soon going to get married. I congratulate her. Meanwhile I tell her about my other two friends Lila and Rinku. She knows them already from the story of my life.

"But you haven't met them?" I tell her.

She looks forward to meet them and I promise her that I will make her meet with them soon.

And then she comes running at me from nowhere. So fast we all have changed and she the most. She looks pretty in white. She ties back her hair. She is perspiring due to heat.

"Look what I got Aama". She tells me in her chirpy voice.

Yes she is my Bhagya, my daughter whom I had struggled so much to give her birth and keep her alive and away from all the troubles that I had faced. Now she has grown up into a beautiful three year old toddler. She shows me what she had got. It is a cotton candy. She tears a piece and pushes it in my mouth. I respond to her sweet gesture with a peck on her cheeks. She looks at Laura and decides whether or not to share the candy with her. And looking at my eyes she tries to get an approval. I blink my eyes and she takes it as a yes. She then gives a bite to Laura. Now she runs away again to play with some of the other kids.

"Your daughter looks just like you." Laura says.

"I often get to hear this from all." I tell her.

I want to talk more about my daughter with her. So I tell her that she loves me a lot. She is an intelligent child and we practice the alphabets together but I lag behind. She is also an interesting story teller and how I wonder the tiny toddler being so efficient in making me smile with her magical stories.

"Her name is indeed meaningful". Laura tells me again.

I tell her the reason behind choosing that particular name for her. It is because I always took her as my lucky charm from the time I conceived her. 'Bhagya' means 'destiny' so for me my daughter is a sign of good luck. She gave me the strength to flee from the brothel. I was so overwhelmed with love that taking risk was the major leap of mine. And yet it opened the gateway of happiness.

We keep talking and Bhagya comes to me again. The conversation did not even make us realise that it was already evening. And then from the bushes we hear the noisy insects.

Bhagya cries out in excitement and begins to clap her hands as she sees a host of fireflies illuminating the darkness where we were. The last rays of the sun dissolve the white clouds and make it look mesmerising. Bhagya holds my hand while Laura intently looks at the sky. I silently praise the creation of God.